# SOLD TO THE HITMAN

## ALEXIS ABBOTT

PATHFORGERS PUBLISHING

Get an EXCLUSIVE book, **FREE** just as a thank you for signing up for my newsletter! Plus you'll never miss a new release, cover reveal, or promotion!

http://alexisabbott.com/newsletter

PART OF ALEXIS ABBOTT'S HITMAN
SERIES

READING ORDER:

Don't miss out on the rest of the Hitman Series by Alexis Abbott! Now available on all ebook retailers, in paperback format, and now becoming available in audiobook!

*Owned by the Hitman*
*Sold to the Hitman*
*Saved by the Hitman*
*Captive of the Hitman*
*Stolen from the Hitman*
*Hostage of the Hitman*
*Taken by the Hitman*

# ANDREI

*I* never feel out of place in the unique stillness that the streets of this city maintains at night. Even if the noise in Brighton Beach keeps on at a dull roar long into the late hours, there's a certain sense in the air that in this little corner of New York, the gears of the city are taking a rest.

And these special hours give me my hunting grounds.

I'm leaning against the brick wall that makes up a side of The Vixen, a gentleman's club that seems to draw just about every man in the city through its doors at least once. Its reputation and popularity have made it a true asset to its owners, my associates of the Bratva — the brotherhood we Russians in Brighton have established.

ALEXIS ABBOTT

The men who come through this club couldn't be more useful. They drink in the front, they gamble in the back, and they're loose with their words in both.

All of this and more is what I suspect my target is doing while I wait for him. I take a drink from the flask in hand and check my watch before glancing around the corner — 2:24 AM. Most of the time I'm faking the swig, but a forlorn-looking *Russkiy* drinking outside a strip club looks less suspicious than a large man waiting outside it with arms crossed. Not that it matters. According to my client, the target should be stumbling out any minute now, and in no state to notice the difference.

And nobody in their right mind would question me.

As if on cue, the man my client wants dead staggers past the haggard-looking bouncer, narrowing his eyes at him as he does. He's got ratty, thin hair tied back in a ponytail that's graying, and he hasn't shaved in a few days, a patchy, greasy beard sticking out from pale cheeks.

"The fuck you lookin' at, ya thin-dicked cock-splatter?" he sneers at the bouncer.

The bouncer just gives him a brief glance before going back to his phone. He has impressive patience. My target spits on the ground and starts off towards his apartment. He's wearing a nice suit that fits him poorly, and it's got visible stains on it. He reeks of sleazy, ill-gotten gains, just as expected. The kind of

2

man who steps on others to get where he's going and makes a fool of himself with the spoils. I wait half a minute before starting after him, silently. The bouncer pays me no mind.

I feel good about this job. That seems to be rarer these days, but this particular hit has a few things going for it — the first being that this sleazebag has it coming.

This is a freelance contract, meaning I'm not being sicced on someone for my boss. My boss is one of the most feared men in Brighton Beach, in part because of how wantonly he doles out violence against people he thinks are his enemies. My last hit was on a man I knew to be innocent — a simple man vaguely tied to the Bratva, but guilty only of making some small slight against my boss.

And if my boss ever discovers how I really handled that job, it will be my name next on his list. The memories flash in my mind's eye.

*I'm tailing the man on his drive to his beach house. He pulls over at a gas station and heads into the bathroom. I leave my car beside the dumpster and head to his. I slip into the backseat and lie down. A few minutes pass, and I hear him open the car door, not suspecting a thing. He pulls out of the gas station, and once he's back on track, speeding to his home, I cock my gun in the backseat.*

I come back to reality with a start, and I remind myself that the man I'm following tonight is no such innocent by any measure. My client was nearly incoherent with fury when he contacted me, so I figured this was something very personal. After I got the essential information from the client, the rest of the story fell into place with only a little digging.

The scum I'm walking twenty paces behind through Brooklyn runs a string of payday loan offices. When he isn't drinking on the job or conning the working-class clients who had to turn to him, he was making advances on one of the poor employees who worked full-time at his office not far from here — my client's sister.

Four days ago, this woman was reported missing. Two days after that, my client contacted me.

He knew what had happened to his sister. Just before disappearing, she had come to him in tears over how her boss had been unusually aggressive in his advances that day, grabbing her and saying unspeakable things to her. She rejected him, and he threatened to fire her. It didn't take a genius to figure out why she disappeared shortly after. But the investigation went impossibly slow; this scumbag had bought men on the local beat. Moreover, he knew the law never cared for the poor folk barely scraping by in the best of cases. So like many helpless souls before him, he turned outside the law.

The other upside to this job is the pay. This is one hundred grand I'll be making with a clean conscience, for whatever my conscience was worth.

The target is ahead of me, still staggering, but I'm

impressed by his ability to keep his eyes forward. Drunks are often easily distracted, but I can tell this is a walk this sod has made many, many times. He has a remarkable ability to shake from his mind that he's guilty of murdering a young woman.

I wonder how his candor would change if he knew this stumble home would be his last.

The target was finally reaching his apartment, and I slowed to a halt and pretended to turn off into an alleyway as he bent over near a storm drain to start puking his guts out. I'm silently thankful I won't have that mess to deal with in a few moments.

As I hear the target stop, I slip out from the alley and watch him head around the apartment building towards his own underground residence. Despite my bulk, I'm able to move behind him like a shadow drawing ever closer.

When I was being trained, my partner at the time thought it was amusing, the sight of such a large man dressed in all black slinking around like a predator. He was the first one to call me *Shadow*, and it seems to have stuck.

Still far enough back that I'm out of sight, I hear the target's keys scrape and clatter on the metal lock as his drunken stupor makes him struggle with the door, and memories of my last job flood back to me.

*He struggles with the lock, his hand shaking violently with fear as he feels the cold barrel of my gun pressed to the back of his head. "Faster!" I bark, and he drops the keys with a whimper. When he finally manages to get the door open, I take him by the scruff of his collar and toss him inside, and he sprawls out onto the floor of the sparsely furnished home he can barely afford. The man is jelly, looking up at me with tear-streaked eyes.*

*"Please, sir!" he gasps, gesturing wildly around the room as if offering its contents to me. "All of this, my house, my car, you can take it all, but please —"*

*I silence him as I put a cloth to his mouth, pressing it tight into his teeth as I lean forward, keeping him from making sudden movements. "Enough talk," I order in a still voice.*

The sound of the clicking lock brings me back to the present, and just like that, it's time to act.

I start to close the distance behind him as he jiggles the knob of the door, pushing it open with a little effort before he stumbles inside when it finally gives way. By the time he's got his bearings back, I'm within arm's reach of the door. When he tries to throw the door shut, it meets only my hand.

"What th-" is all he has time to get out before I'm on him, the cloth in my hand muffling his scream as I press it into his mouth, holding the back of his head in the other. He's too startled to resist me as I spin him around, forcing him to the ground with a sharp kick to the back of his knees. His legs give out easily.

I kick the door shut with a quick motion. He's starting to jerk around under me, and I know I don't have much time. The couch is next to the door. In a fluid motion, I grab one of the stained pillows and press his head into the ground, cloth in his mouth, and I cover his head with the pillow.

The next instant, I draw my pistol from the back of my belt, a silencer placed upon the tip of the barrel, and I aim it at the pillow.

Two quiet thumps of the silenced bullets hitting the pillow, and the target's struggling stops.

I stand up from the man's lifeless body as blood begins to trickle out from under the cushion. I reach over to a blanket draped across the back of the couch and toss it over the man's body. He won't be missed.

*"More will come for you if they don't think you're dead," I tell the cowering man as he looks at me incredulously. I'm looking him dead in the eye, speaking carefully, as if giving instructions to a child. That's all this poor man is in the world of the mafia. "I know you to be innocent. My boss does not care, but I do."*

*He claps his hands together as if in prayer, putting his forehead to them. "God bless you, sir, I can never —" But I cut him off.*

*"I have a safe house. I will take you there, and I will have food brought to you until it is safe for you to leave the country — that's all there is left for you now. Start anew. You will be thought dead. You won't be missed."*

I push the memories away once more. That hit was going to be the last time I ever found myself in such a position. That day, as I spirited away that innocent man to a safe place, I vowed to know the character of my targets. If I was to be an executioner, I must also play the judge.

I look down at the man I've just killed. Blood is starting to soak through the blanket. Without another word, I push open the door with my gloved hands, closing it behind me and sealing away that wretched man in the pigsty where he made his lair.

As I head out around the dark apartment building, I pull my jacket collar up and lower my head. I don't suspect the cameras here — if there are any — mind one shadowy figure moving around any more than another, but I'm not taking chances.

I walk down the sidewalk away from the scene as if I'm heading home after a routine walk. The streets are nearly empty, save for a stray car that drives by with a slight swerve, a few of them probably from The Vixen.

I pay them no mind. This has become routine for me. My eyes turn toward the moonless sky, and I wonder how many other people in the city lead lives so nocturnal they can tell when the new moon is just a little brighter than usual.

Hours roll on as I walk around the city — heading straight back to my car after a hit would be a rookie mistake. By the time I'm strolling back to the parking lot of The Vixen, orange light is piercing the skyline, and I glance up at the sunrise as I open my car door. It brings me back to the midnight sun back in Siberia, where the star's icy light was a mocking comfort.

No time to reminisce now, though. I've got a client to report to.

CASSIE

*I*'m sitting in my room, staring out the window at the little red and brown birds hopping along the branches of our magnolia tree. They're chirping so sweetly and happily, and I wonder what kind of conversation they must be having. *What do little red birds talk about?* I ponder, resting my chin on my arms. If only I could understand them. I can't help fantasizing about what it must be like to fly.

It's six in the morning and the sun is just starting to peek its bulbous golden face from behind the skyline of my suburban neighborhood, the homes all nearly identical, like a neighborhood of doll houses. Last night, there was a storm, so my father crowded us all into the den to watch the lightning and talk about the power of God. He does this every time a particularly nasty storm rolls through. He just wants us all to appreciate how small and insignificant we are, teach us to fear our inevitable smiting by the almighty if we succumb to sin. Daddy tells me that every time lightning strikes the ground, it is retribution for a sin committed in that spot. From this, I can gather that there is a whole lot of sinning going on.

We live in upstate New York, in a tiny little town full of beautiful parks and trees. There are lovely forests and lakes, but I don't get out to see them very often. My parents know how dangerous it is out there, so they try their best to protect me from it and keep me locked up inside.

Sometimes this makes me sad. But I know it is a sin to defy one's parents or to think negative thoughts about them. So I just remind myself that they are only trying to keep me safe from temptation, to keep me clean of sin.

Today is my eighteenth birthday, and I am graduating from the homeschooling program I've spent my entire life studying. It is bittersweet, saying goodbye to the textbooks and lessons which have given me glimpses, albeit obscured, of the outside world. From my geography books, I learned about just how huge the Earth is. And from my parents, I have learned just how evil most of that world really is. They have taught me that anything outside the little social group we've cultivated is tainted, too dangerous. Everyone in our group feels just as strongly about what Daddy says, and the one time someone dared disagree with the world view of the group, they weren't invited back anymore.

Sometimes, the pictures in my textbooks make me feel some kind of strange wanderlust. But any sort of lust is utterly forbidden, even if it's only a longing for another place, a piece of scenery I have never known. The world is filled with amazing colors I've never even touched, but I must remind myself that beauty like that can surely only be the devil's work, trying to tempt me to step into a sinful world.

I glance at the clock. Any second now my mother will come and knock on my door, letting me know that it's time to get up. Oversleeping is a symptom of laziness, an indicator of a slothful, ungrateful attitude.

And sloth is a deadly sin.

But they've frightened me enough that I always wake up before my mother even comes to get me. I want more than anything to be the best daughter I can be. I need to be perfect. And lately, my parents have been telling me that soon I'll need to be more than just a perfect daughter.

I need to be the perfect wife.

There's a curt knock at my bedroom door and I hear my mother's voice call out, "Time to get up, Cassie. Get dressed and come down to make breakfast."

"Yes, Mother!" I reply cheerily.

I jump up from my little spot by the window, my knee-length, white eyelet night dress swirling as I rise to my feet. I flounce over to the gray wooden vanity in the corner of my room, sitting down on the rickety stool. My face blinks back at me in the round mirror, and I can't stifle a yawn. I do like rising early, but lately I haven't been sleeping very well. This is subtly reflected in the light shadows beneath my eyes. I know my father will comment on this. The slightest flaw in my appearance is an affront to God, who made me. I need to be wholesome and beautiful, and this means I must be perfect at all times.

Especially if I am to be someone's wife!

I lean closer and scrutinize my smooth, pale skin, looking for any imperfections. But luckily, I have been blessed with exceptionally clear skin. My mother says it's because I am so faithful to my God, but I personally, secretly believe it has more to do with genetics — something I read in a science book before my father confiscated it. Of course, I would never admit that, though.

My cheeks are tinged rosy pink, and my full lips part in a perfectly symmetrical, straight smile, dimples appearing on both cheeks. I have long lashes framing my large, pale blue eyes, but I have never worn mascara on them. In fact, I've never worn any kind of makeup. It is forbidden in my household. Sometimes, at the supermarket, I have sneaked away from my mother to look at the makeup aisles, in complete awe of the multitudes of colors and textures. I know nothing about how makeup is supposed to be worn, but the colorful shades of lipstick have always intrigued me.

I wonder if I will be allowed to wear colors like that on my wedding day. I assume not, as the husband my parents choose for me will probably be a likeminded individual, carefully selected from our tight-knit, closed-off social group. My parents have a lot of friends, all from the congregation at church. Most of them are also parents who homeschool their children. At church I have stolen glances at these other young people, some of them around my age. I wonder if they are just as restricted as me. I think they must be. Children are meant to be seen and not heard, though, so I don't have many opportunities to speak with them.

During the last church service we attended, I surveyed the crowded pews, looking for male faces. I wanted to see what the pool of potential husbands looked like. I was dismayed to see how dull and plain they all were. I know that men don't need to be handsome to serve God. But women must be beautiful, because the best way that a woman can serve God is by serving her husband. Therefore, a woman must be both beautiful and pure.

At least, that's what my father and mother have told me.

Perched in front of the mirror, I comb my waist-length, silvery blonde hair over my shoulder, working the tangles out of my soft curls. Then I plait it down my back in a simple, no-nonsense braid that keeps my hair out of my face. I get up and stand in front of my armoire, trying to decide what I should wear today.

Finally, I settle on an ankle-length light pink skirt, beige button-up blouse, and a chocolate brown cardigan. The pink skirt is the brightest article of clothing I own, and I hope that my eighteenth birthday is a fitting occasion to wear it. My parents usually only buy me muted neutral tones, like gray and brown. A woman is not meant to be flashy for anyone but her husband and her God. I think about the little red and brown birds outside on the branches. The lady bird is brown and the male is bright red. My father says this is proof that women are meant to be modest and men are to be powerful.

After I smooth down my skirt and make sure that most of my flesh is covered up, I go down the hall to tap on my little brother's door and wake him up. Isaiah is seven years old and the sweetest child in the world, I'm convinced. He is rowdy sometimes, of course, but Father says that is acceptable for little boys. Girls are supposed to be soft and quiet, but boys can be loud and messy. It's just the way things are.

"It's time to get up, Isaiah," I say through the door.

I hear him groan and roll out of bed, and I smile to myself as I walk down the stairs and into the kitchen. My mother is already there, wearing a long brown dress and white apron. Her blonde hair is tied back into a perfectly round bun, as usual. She radiates a kind of demure, sophisticated beauty that I aspire to. She takes me on a lot of outings to have tea or coffee with other mother-daughter pairs from church. I think she wants to let me see a little bit of the world, even if it is only a sliver.

"Good morning, Mother," I greet her, taking my place beside her at the kitchen island. She is rolling out dough for homemade biscuits, and there's a frying pan of bacon and eggs on the stove across from us.

"Happy birthday," she replies. "Could you take over these biscuits so I can tend the stove?"

"Of course!" I say, taking an apron from a peg on the wall and tying it around my neck and waist. It certainly wouldn't do to have my clean outfit covered in flour.

"And hurry, please. Your father is in quite a rush this morning. He has a meeting with some, uh, business partners in a couple hours."

"Yes, Mother." I quickly and efficiently form the biscuits, arranging them on a baking sheet and pop them into the oven. Then I gather a stack of cloth napkins and four sets of silverware to set the table. My brother and father both take a lot longer to come down in the morning, but that's okay. My mother and I are made to serve, and we do it happily.

She was married to my father when she was eighteen and he was thirty, and despite the fact that they did not know each other until the day of their wedding, they have made a lovely life together. My mother is very subservient and very good at maintaining a beautiful house. Our two-story craftsman home is furnished with refurbished antique furniture and hand-sewn linens, and my mother keeps it perfectly spotless at all times. "A woman's home is reflective of her soul," she always tells me, "So keep it clean."

Once all the food is cooked, we place portions on each plate and fill the glasses with freshly-squeezed orange juice, just in time for my father and Isaiah to come down the stairs, rough-housing playfully. Standing primly by his chair to pull it out for him, I greet my father.

"Good morning, Daddy," I say, smiling widely.

He is a tall, broad-shouldered man with a thick mustache and beard, once brown and now gray peppered with white. He's dressed in a dark business suit and tie, everything perfectly polished and ironed smooth, from his slacks to his cuff links. He is an investment banker, and from what I have gathered, a very powerful man in our community. All the time, women at church tell my mother how lucky she is to have landed such a prestigious man. But all of her thanks go to God, of course.

"Good morning, and happy birthday," he says, his voice deep and resonant.

Isaiah's face lights up. "It's your birthday?" he asks excitedly.

I nod. "Yes! I'm eighteen today."

He gasps and bolts toward me, flinging his arms around my waist and hugging me tightly. I laugh and ruffle his fluffy brown hair. He is a handful, to be sure, but he is never dull. In fact, some days I shudder to think how boring and quiet my life would be without him running around. I'm going to miss him terribly when I get married. But I'm sure I will still see him all the time, especially since my husband is almost certainly going to be a part of our established community here.

"Eighteen? That's so old!" Isaiah bursts out, peering up at me with a wrinkled nose.

I kiss the top of his head. "I know. I'm ancient now."

"Does this mean Cassie's gonna go away?" he asks, turning to my father with a suddenly worried expression. He clings to my hand, pressing his chubby little cheek into my palm.

My heart tightens in my chest at how panicked he sounds. My parents are wonderful, of course, but it hurts me to think of my little brother being all alone in the house without me there to entertain and take care of him. My mother is home all the time, and she looks after him, but she doesn't play with him like I do. Apart from a couple neighborhood boys, I am Isaiah's best friend in the world. I hope he won't be too lonely without me.

My parents exchange concerned glances. Then my mother takes Isaiah by the hand and takes him to his seat quietly.

"Perhaps we will discuss this over breakfast," Daddy says, scratching at his beard. Suddenly, I feel a little fearful. They're acting a little peculiar.

"I won't be going too far, I'm sure," I tell Isaiah with a wink as I take my seat across from him at the table. My parents sit down and we all eat in silence for a couple minutes, waiting for my father to speak.

Finally, he sets his fork and knife down and announces, "We have selected a husband for you, Cassandra."

I nearly choke on my biscuit.

"Already?" I ask, my eyes going wide. I hadn't expected an announcement quite this big this morning. I thought they would take a lot longer to pick a candidate, and I had hoped — a very small, quiet hope — that they would include me in the decision to some extent. I know it isn't my place to choose; my parents know what is best for me, anyway. But I don't know if I am ready to be anyone's wife. Not quite yet.

"No!" shouts Isaiah.

"Hush, sweetheart," my mother tells him softly, shaking her head at him.

But my brother slams down his fork and crosses his arms. "I don't want Cassie to go!"

"It is nothing to fear," my father tells Isaiah firmly. "And it is none of your business. It is an arrangement between your sister and... God."

"Could you tell me his name?" I ask, my hands starting to tremble. I look back and forth between my parents as they give each other knowing looks.

"Um, no. We... we can't," my mother says.

"Don't worry about it," says my father.

Now my stomach is turning in knots. Why are they acting so strangely? Why is my future husband's name such a big secret? I have probably already heard his name in passing — our community is very exclusive, and everyone knows everybody else.

"Haven't I met him before?" I press, daring to test my father's patience in my panic.

"N-no, you have not," Mother answers hesitantly. My father shoots her a warning glare and her mouth closes tight.

Daddy clears his throat and folds his hands on the table in front of him, pushing his plate forward as he fixes me with a dark gaze. "It is not your place to question our judgement in this matter, Cassandra. Put your faith in God, where it belongs, and do not fret about your fate. Rest assured that this deci-

ALEXIS ABBOTT

sion will be made based on what is best for our family."

I stare quietly down at my plate, my appetite totally dissipated by now. I feel as though I'm on the verge of tears, but crying is not allowed in front of other people, and especially not in my father's presence. I resign myself to crying later, alone in my room. But before I drop the subject entirely, I ask one more question: "So, he is of our faith, then?"

My father pauses, and a shadowy darkness crosses his face. I am afraid of him in that instant, as I often am. I love Daddy, but sometimes he frightens me with his sternness.

Then he replies, "We don't know."

My mouth falls open before I can stop it, and tears burn in my eyes, threatening to spill over. But I cannot let them. So I swallow my fear, nod my understanding, and quietly remind myself that I must trust my parents.

Surely they would never send me away somewhere bad. They have protected me from evil all my life — so I must continue to trust them now.

It's what a good girl would do.

# ANDREI

*N*obody pays attention to the droves of men slipping into the back room of the little store on the street corner. Very few of the regular patrons of the grocery and cafe aren't Russian, and none of the locals know about this place. It's the worst-kept secret in Little Odessa.

The back room of the store sports a narrow staircase that leads to a basement that's far larger than the building, and it's what's really keeping this sorry excuse for a Russian cafe afloat.

It's a dimly-lit place lined with yellow, flickering lights that cast a cheap, unkempt feel about the whole place, but really, the security at tonight's event is a testament to how valuable it is to the *Bratva*. Enough money has passed through this shoddy-looking basement to buy out most of this part of town.

I'm standing at the bottom of the stairs, keeping my eyes on the men who are shuffling in. They come from all walks of life, from surly-looking men in stained tanktops to a few gentlemen in designer clothing. I recognize a few of them, but I'm in neither the mood nor position to make small talk with old acquaintances. There's a makeshift bar set up at the far corner of the room, and more than a few of the people who've been here a while are already getting drunk.

I'm wearing a tight-fitting black shirt and jeans, nothing fancy for tonight. Dressing more simply makes the dregs less likely to think about fucking with me.

Bouncing isn't the kind of gig I like, but I know my boss assigned me to this post since I've been in minimal contact with him the past week or so. He's the kind of man who demands regular attention. Not unlike a child.

Of course, if he's so interested in things going smoothly tonight that he has a hitman handling security, something high-stakes must be happening tonight. Poker games are a popular one, and I've seen more than a few of Brighton's highest-profile businessmen and criminals alike lose fortunes under these lights.

High-dollar drugs aren't out of the question either, but I find it doubtful with all the people here.

Back in the 80s, though, I can imagine this place saw its share of coke parties.

I see a few burly men making their way down the stairs, and I give them a nod of recognition, knowing whose guard dogs they are. A moment later, their master — my boss — makes his way down the stairs wearing a lavish and gaudy orange jacket and a thick gold chain, laughing with what looks like a similarly dressed Chechnyan from across town.

"Ah, and here is the man who'll keep us sleeping safe at night," he gestures to me as he reaches the bottom of the stairs where I'm standing cross-armed, a statue compared to the other guards. "My own personal *Shadow* — I couldn't replace this man with a hundred of these other goons, I tell you!"

"Mr. Slokavich," I incline my head to him, "You and your friends have something special planned for the night?"

"Andrei," he chides me, slapping me on the back heartily, "have I ever hosted something that disappoints? Sergei Slokavich is not a man to let his valued guests go wanting, you of all people know this."

*He's trying to suck up to someone*, I think privately, giving a smile to Sergei and his rich friend. Sergei is a proud man, but sucking up when it's useful is not beneath him by any measure. Tonight must be something special indeed.

"People are still buzzing over last week's match," I

agree, bringing up the fixed fight Sergei had a chubby hand in. "It takes a special talent to draw men from all walks of life like this."

"Aahh," Sergei says, holding up a finger triumphantly. I've learned how to flatter him fairly easily over the years. "Good eye as ever — you see?" He turns to his Chechnyan friend again, who's looking bemused. "This is why he's my best. Ace in the hole, the Americans call it. And he's absolutely right, tonight is going to be something for the whole community. Now come along," Sergei starts to wander into the crowd with his wealthy friend, "there are a few of my associates who've been dying to meet you, and..."

His voice trails off as he and his men melt into the crowd, and I'm left alone again. *Finally.*

Working for Sergei Slokavich has become more of a chore over time. When he isn't having half the other Russians in Brighton Beach killed, he's indulging in every vice he can lay his hands on. Embarrassing as he is from my point of view, I have to admit, he's skilled at making friends with deep pockets, particularly those who are fresh off the boat from the motherland.

The Chechnyan with him put on airs of authority, and judging by his age, I guess he's the absurdly wealthy son of some mob boss back home, but even though we all spoke Russian, I could tell from his silence that he hardly spoke a word of the English that was being chattered all around him by the rabble. He's out of his element, and Sergei is taking the chance to butter him up. It's a clever ploy, but I wonder how long it'll last.

I don't have long to think about it, as the lights start to dim and focus on the stage at the far end of the room and people start to gather around.

That stage has been used to auction off high-dollar stolen goods in the past. I've seen everything from filched art and antiques to military-grade custom weapons pass through that stage. Whatever Sergei is selling tonight, it's going to be good. I don't have to crane my neck to see over the sea of people in the room.

A blonde man with a tight goatee I recognize stands up on the stage, running a hand through his hair as he waves at the crowd to quiet them, obviously playing the auctioneer for tonight. I chuckle.

The man's name is Oskar, and he's been through the ringer with the Bratva. Used to be a fairly successful collector until being recently disgraced by a job that went bad. I had been wondering where he'd end up after that kind of shame.

"Quiet down, quiet down!" he shouts at the crowd, "Gentlemen, you'll want every one of your senses free for what we've got tonight!" One of the other bouncers reaches up from below to hand him a mic, and he grins, trying to look dramatic. He always was a fast talker.

"I see all the faces in this room have come from far and wide, and tonight's entertainment does too! I got an eyeful of what we've got in store for you, and let me tell you, I envy those of you with the deepest pockets out there! But don't worry, these goods have never before been sampled!"

There's a dark laughter that goes out around the crowd of men, and I arch an eyebrow, getting a bad feeling about where he's going with this.

"But you didn't come to hear me ramble, so without further ado," he turns to stage left and waggles his finger in a repulsive beckoning gesture, "come on out, ladies!"

With some hesitation and encouragement from the musclebound goon behind them, ten young women stumble out onto the stage, and the crowd starts hooting and hollering.

Immediately, I feel rage burning in my heart. Each one of the women is scantily clad, a few of them outfitted in counterfeits of expensive lingerie, others wearing nothing more than star or heart-shaped nipple coverings and underwear.

Every terrified young woman, none of them a day over 20 and all of them shaking with wide-eyed fear at the sea of ravenous, drunk men cheering up at them, holds a little placard with a number on it.

This is a slave auction.

My hands ball into fists, and I feel my face going red. So this is what Sergei valued so dearly that he wanted his best man guarding it — a flesh trade, the most lowly and vile practice even the Bratva could sink to.

My first impulse is to consider how easy it could be to kill all of these disgusting pigs in the room. My stints in Russian prisons taught me quickly how to size up a crowd of surly men that far outnumber you. A crowd of drunks like this was no comparison to a prison full of abusive, slave-driving guards and broken prisoners.

If it weren't for the risk to the innocent young women up on stage, I would go through with it, but I can tell by the looks on their faces that none of them have so much as seen a drunk, belligerent man, much less be held up like a piece of meat for a crowd of them.

"Here they are!" Oskar announces, striding around, eyeing each one of the ladies up and down. "Each of them unspoiled, each of them eighteen, each of them *very* eager to please! Here," he says, stopping at the girl with the "#1" placard, reading off a card in his hand, "we have a lovely young lady from out west in California! She's a lifelong hiker and health nut, and it's clearly paid off!" He gestures up and down the woman's legs as the crowd cheers.

Oskar goes on in such a fashion, introducing each lady and getting the crowd whipped up into a lustful frenzy. As he goes down the row of women, I start to turn my eyes away in disgust when I notice the woman standing towards the far end of the stage.

She stands out from the rest of the women on stage like a ray of warm sunshine. Clad in nothing but a simple white bra and panties, her knees are turned inward as she uses her placard, #7, as if trying to hide behind it. Her luminous blue eyes are full of fear they should never be exposed to, and two blonde braids hang over her shoulders, gracing pale skin that's pure as porcelain. She's small and fragile-looking, even more so than the others on stage, like a doll being held up before a pack of wolves.

She's the most beautiful women I've ever seen.

"And here," Oskar says as he reaches her, taking her by the arm and dragging her in front of the other girls, snapping me out of the trance I'd been in gazing at her, "here we have a real gem from the north part of our very own state! Azure eyes, golden hair, and a body you can toss around the bed as long as she lasts!"

Hearing Oskar talk about that angel as he did makes me forget my post. I stride forward, pushing past some of the crowd as easily as if I were wading through tall grass. I want to get up on stage and throttle him, but I notice Sergei and his friends up front, and I use every ounce of my strength to restrain myself.

"She's domestically trained, a true angel of the house," he croons, stalking around her like a demon as she shrinks away from him. "Never so much as felt a man's touch before, and the only condition of this perfect servant being yours and yours alone is a wedding ring! That's right, gentleman, the highest bidder gets this little doll sent away to her parents for a few days to get dressed and groomed for you and nobody else, for life!"

The men go wild, obviously ravenous with lust, and I can see a few of the more affluent-looking men looking poised, ready to pounce. For many of them, I realize, this woman would be the deal of a lifetime — a perfect wife to legitimize their images, and one who won't pry or ask questions, either.

Oskar moves through the other women, but I can already hear men around me chattering over #7.

"I'll deflower that pretty little rose."

"Not like my kid's going to college, I'd cough up those funds to fuck that little bitch!"

"Looks kinda like my daughter, gimme a piece of that ass to tear up!"

The poor girl looks absolutely terrified, her eyes flitting from man to man as they shout at her, and she tries to back away, but Oskar casts her a dark look, and she bites her lip nervously, knees shaking.

"Hey! Hey, #7! Want a real man to help you stretch those pretty lips of yours?"

The last man at my right makes me forget my restraint, and I turn to grab him by the scruff of his neck, taking him off-guard and terrifying him as I

31

pulled him close to me, about to knock him to the ground when Oskar's voice boomed.

"Alright, boys, alright settle down! You've seen the ladies, now let's see the offers! Start the bidding!"

Both of us were distracted by the shouts we started hearing from around us, and I dropped the man to listen.

"Gimme #7! Fifty thousand!" cried a desperate-looking man who looked like he could barely afford the counterfeit watch around his wrist.

"Our first bidder in at fifty grand," Oskar shouted, and two-thirds of the crowd groaned at the lowball offer. Most girls can net over a hundred thousand a year as a sex slave, wedding ring or no.

"Seventy-five!" shouted a man wearing a high-collared coat and wide-brimmed hat as not to be seen. The girl is looking at each bidder in alarm. The poor woman has probably never even faced a date with a man, much less this animalistic show.

"One-fifty," comes the calm, firm voice of an older man in a tailored Armani suit.

"One seventy-five," cries another man I recognize as a human trafficker. I can't let this go on any longer. Any of the men in this room bidding at this threshold are with the likes of criminals too wealthy to know kindness anymore. They're not buying her for their own pleasure, and I know what this is going to lead to. The wealthy men in fine outfits are no less crude than the mongrels that were jeering at her earlier — they only have the power to go through with those words.

Before I realize what I'm doing, I muscle my way to the front of the stage and shout out an offer.

"Three-hundred thousand!"

I've only felt that many eyes turn to me a couple of other times in my life, and never with such hostility. Even Oskar seemed stunned for a moment, stammering before echoing my offer.

"Th-three hundred from the man in black! Finally, we're getting some real offers on the go!"

"Three-fifty," came a bark from a new voice, and I looked over to see Sergei's wealthy young Chechnyan standing up for the bid. Sergei was giving me a warning look, but I wasn't in the mood to be jerked around by him tonight. I looked up at the stage and glared Oskar in the eye.

"Six hundred." A few moments of silence pass, and I can feel stunned eyes on me all around the room, including one from the young lady I'd just bid several men's lives' worth of work on.

Every time the Chechnyan bid, I upped the ante. I couldn't believe it, not with how my boss kept staring daggers at me. I was cutting off my source of income while at the same time laying down months of hard, dangerous work.

And then, a half-dozen bids later, they're defeated.

"We have a winner at one point six million! And

yes, this is in American!" Oskar nearly splutters when it was clear nobody dared outbid me. "This young lady is all yours, my good man! Meet the boys out front to settle the details, aaaaand we're off to a rolling start! Now then, we still have nine lovely ladies who…"

I turn and push my way towards the stairs as Oskar starts to drone on with the rest of the auction, my heart still pounding furiously.

*Did I really just drop over one-and-a-half-million dollars on that woman?*

As I push my way towards the back, I hear one of the men who had been jeering at the girl spit, and I hear him mutter to another loudly, "Didn't think they let *the help* place bids at these things."

"Hope he gets his fucking money out of it — for that much, I'd make a cum-slut out of that bitch all over New York State."

Without a second thought, my body whirls around like lightning, my fist flying out and cracking the second man on the jaw. A moment later, he hits the ground, out cold.

Before the people around me can react, the man's friend lurches at me, but I catch him with a quick punch to the gut, doubling him over, and with a quick crack to the back of the head with my elbow, I send him to the ground with his friend.

Up on the stage, Oskar is trying desperately to keep the audience's attention, but many of the men

SOLD TO THE HITMAN

are staring at me now. A few of them might have been thinking about jumping into the brawl, but my quick end to the hecklers seems to make them think twice. I cast them all a steely gaze before hearing a groan from one of the men I'd just dropped.

Kneeling down, I take him by the collar with one hand.

"Speak so crudely about a woman again in my presence, and it'll be the last words out of the few teeth you have left," I warn him.

Standing up, I glance at the men staring at the scene. "What are the lot of you looking at? Don't you have a meat market to enjoy?"

Without looking back, I make my way up the stairs, and the other patrons give me a wide berth. I don't look back, even though I can feel many eyes on me — Sergei's, his wealthy friend's, the bidders', and even the young woman's.

Nobody pays me much mind as I cross through the cafe and out onto the streets. None of them heard anything, I imagine. But as I start to head down the street, my head still buzzing over everything that's happened.

I'd disobeyed orders, embarrassed Sergei Slokavich in front of more than a few wealthy friends, and abandoned my post.

More importantly, I'd just sealed my marriage to a young woman I didn't even know. A woman whose first impression of me was beating two men to the ground without breaking a sweat.

*I just bought a marriage.* What in the hell was I thinking? I swear under my breath, running a hand through my hair as I walk. I had wanted to spare her, but instead, I bound her to a contract assassin for life. The money was no issue — it was a little more than a dozen jobs' worth, sure, but I had more where that came from. Besides, jobs outside the Bratva tend to pay better, and I might not be their most favorite person right now.

But marriage? I've never even come close to considering such a thing. Both in Russia and in the States, I've had plenty of fun with women, but married life doesn't pair with my line of work.

Yet when the thought comes to mind, I can't help but remember the sight of her up there, far too cold and alone for a ray of sunshine as beautiful and innocent-looking as her. I run a hand over my face, though, as I remember that she saw me strike down those two drunks — a harmless lamb's first impression of the *Shadow* who now owns her.

The reminder hits me like a punch to the gut. If the poor girl was afraid enough tonight, how terrified must she be now?

The three days leading up to my wedding have been the worst days of my life.

I have been holed up in my room as much as possible, my eyes wide and my lips sealed shut, too afraid to say anything to anyone. I probably haven't said more than two words per day. My parents have dragged me around by the arm, from the wedding cake tasting to the dress fitting. As I stood on the little round platform being poked and prodded by the seamstress, my mother fidgeted awkwardly and my father pointed out all the areas where my skin could be seen. Even the most conservative dress in the bridal boutique was still too risque for my father's tastes, as he agitatedly pointed out to the seamstress my exposed collarbone, forearms, and back. The dress was more akin to a prom dress in style, with a princessy, lacy corset top and a huge, fluffy skirt with layers upon layers of taffeta and tulle. The seamstress assured my father that she could easily and quickly sew in lace inserts to cover any exposed flesh.

"We don't want her to parade down the aisle with her body on display for all the guests to see, of course," explained my father. The seamstress nodded and gave him the same kind of smile everyone gave him — ready to obey. He was a scary man.

"Yes, her body is only for her husband to see. And God, of course," my mother added.

As though the pair of them hadn't just made me strip nearly naked and stand exposed before a group of rowdy, dirty, foul men in some basement of a Russian grocery and cafe.

The contradiction of these experiences blows my mind, still.

I can't believe how hypocritical my parents really are. My whole life, they have treated me like a puritanical princess. But the second the clock ticked midnight on my eighteenth birthday, they suddenly decided to turn me into some kind of whore, to be bought and sold, traded away like chattel.

Sitting in the back seat of my father's white Lincoln town car in my huge, poufy white dress, I have to fight back the tears that have been threatening to overtake me for days. As of yet, I've managed to keep myself from crying. Though, to be fair, that may have more to do with the fact that I've spent the past few days in a state of near-catatonic shock.

After all, before the other night, I was never even alone in a room with a male other than my father or Isaiah. Nobody has seen me naked, or even close, since I was a very small child. And then, to suddenly be surrounded by howling, lustful men in a dank room… it's more than I can take.

I swallow back the lump in my throat and stare down at my newly-manicured hands folded in my lap. I had never been to a nail salon before, and under normal circumstances I might have even enjoyed it. The bright lights and endless selection of colors (though my mother insisted upon my getting a simple, classic French manicure) and the pop music playing in the background would have been truly exciting, otherwise. But under the circumstances, I merely sat limply at the manicure station, my eyes glazed over as the woman chatted gleefully with my mother beside me.

We are now en route to the church we've been attending since before I can remember, and I am nervous about seeing all the familiar faces there. Normally, I would have no reason to fear such a thing. The people of our congregation and the surrounding community all know me so well, know my family. I always dreamed that I would marry within this circle and that my wedding day would be filled with flowers and hymns and smiling faces.

Of course, it is likely that the flowers and hymns and smiling faces will be there.

But now, I will be constantly wondering if they know.

What if they all know what I did? What my family put me through? Will they judge me for marrying a man outside the community? All I know of him is his steely, albeit handsome, face and the fact that he has money — and lots of it. More than I ever realized one person could have.

Oh, and the fact that he has no problem using extreme violence to make a point.

I shudder to think what those clenched fists can do to me, if he so easily knocked a grown, rough-looking man to the ground. I want to believe that my parents would never shove me into a dangerous corner with someone who might hurt me. But after what happened the other night, my faith in both my parents and, dare I say it, my God, has been shaken. I want so badly to trust in them, to believe in a God who will protect me from darkness.

But it is difficult to feel anything but heartbreak and terror at the moment.

When the town car pulls up to the church, there are already smartly-dressed attendees milling about on the front lawn of the church. Our little chapel lies on the top of a hill down a dirt road, and the view overlooks the city below. In my many years coming here week after week, I have always found this outlook to be one of the utmost beauty. Somehow, being elevated above the hustle and bustle of our little town has always made me feel closer to Heaven.

Today, though, I only want to stare down at the ground morosely.

The guests clap excitedly, gasping in awe at the sight of me as my father helps me out of the car. My mother and Isaiah get out first, both dressed neatly in dark green. My father is wearing a black suit and dark green tie, and my mother's dress is long and floaty. I wonder if dark green is supposed to be one of my wedding colors.

I don't know because they have never asked me my preferences.

Besides, it hardly matters. Ever since the events of the other night, I have lost all interest in this wedding. My own wedding. I feel so numb, so broken up inside, that I can hardly force myself to smile when everyone rushes up to hug me and offer their congratulations.

But when Daddy fixes me with one of his notorious warning glares, I remember my position as a sort of diplomat for the family. Everything I do, every move I make, every word I say, reflects on the reputation of my family, and my father will not stand for anything less than perfection. In this case, it means I must proceed through the motions and rituals of my wedding as though I truly want to be here.

Even though I want nothing more than to curl up in a ball and cry.

My husband-to-be is nowhere to be seen, and I suspect this is intentional. My father knows how incongruous he is with the rest of the community. He's an outsider, something our community has always looked at with suspicion and scorn. So the best option is to keep the congregation's contact with him as limited as possible.

I don't mind. I don't want to see him anyway.

As far as I am concerned, any man who would attend an auction in which women are being sold like common cattle is not a man I want to marry. Not that I have a choice.

I know, deep down, that this must be what God wants for me. I have to believe that, otherwise I will be forced to rethink everything I have ever known.

"Congratulations, Cassandra! You make a beautiful bride!" exclaims one of the girls from church, Ruth-Ann. I know she is probably a little jealous. After all, she is twenty years old and still unmarried. In our circle, that is almost unheard of.

"Thank you," I say, with a gracious smile.

She takes my hands, leans in, and asks in a hushed voice, "You must be so excited! I had no idea you were even engaged..."

I remember now. She is relatively new to our

circle and she probably isn't quite accustomed to the idea of arranged marriages yet. That's why she isn't married yet.

"It has happened very fast," I admit, glancing around a little anxiously. I don't want my father to see me talking too much about the details of this arrangement. I assume he isn't particularly open to sharing just how my husband and I met.

Though, for all I know, this *is* the usual ritual. I have attended several weddings in my eighteen years, and for all the world they looked like normal events. But then again, they all looked very much like this one. Like mine.

How am I to know whether or not the other girls were put through the same meat market setup I was? I think back over all the weddings I've gone to. There was the union of Naomi and Jonah just a couple months ago. Naomi looked so happy, so complete, standing next to her tall, skinny new husband Jonah. Had she been forced into a room half-naked with a bunch of drooling, shouting men, too?

Probably not, I assume, since Jonah has been part of the congregation for years. No. They met the old-fashioned way, and now every time I see them at church they are hand-in-hand, always smiling, leaning on each other.

Tears prickle in my eyes again. I want that.

Is this how my father met my mother? He is

much older than her… The thought sends a chill down my spine, though there is a passing reassurance. They still live a Godly life, after all, and mother seems happy and well taken care of…

I look out over the crowds and think to myself just how little I know about the man I am about to marry. I remember his stern profile, his enormous height and thick-shouldered build. His deep, foreboding voice reverberates in my head. He made an impact on me, and was by far the most handsome that I saw in the room. Maybe the most handsome man I'd seen in my life. But what do his good looks hide?

Suddenly, my father's firm hand appears on my shoulder. He leans down to whisper into my ear, "Remember who you represent today."

I have the strange, foreign desire to cry, to scream at him. This is my wedding day! I don't know very much about marriage or about much of anything, really, but I do know that brides are supposed to feel good on days like this! But instead, I want to crumple to the grassy earth and go to sleep, to do anything that will make the world spin away into oblivion.

However, my sense of familial duty overwhelms me, and I simply reply, "Yes, Daddy."

His iron fist tightens on my shoulder, causing me to wince a little. I love my father, and I know he surely only wants what is best for me. But sometimes he does hurt me. I want nothing more than to please him and make him approve of me, to get through this day unscathed by him. I follow his line of sight to the roadside, where a black car has just pulled up. It is an extremely luxurious-looking vehicle, shining and reflective, with very dark windows. I wonder what could be hiding behind the tinted windows.

Then it hits me.

It must be my new husband's car. I see a muscle clench in Daddy's jaw and his eyes go narrow, into dark slits. "He is here," my father says quietly.

"Oh," I breathe, my heart rate quickening.

"You must not betray anything. Don't let anyone see your fear, Cassandra. Remember that your actions reflect on the family, and if you screw this up, you will ruin us all," he explains quickly in an undertone. "Act naturally."

I want to shoot back, *What exactly qualifies as natural in this situation?* But I bite my tongue, as I have always done.

"Yes, Daddy," I say dejectedly.

The overlapping, excited conversations among the crowds have dissipated and now they are only whispering and pointing at the big black car. I suddenly feel very dizzy and I realize that I haven't had much to eat or drink for the past few days. My head starts to go fuzzy, but my father's vice grip on my shoulder holds me up.

Then the driver side door of the car opens up and out steps the man I am to marry.

I don't even get much of a chance to gawk, because my mother and father rush over to herd me into the chapel. "He cannot see you before the ceremony! It's against tradition!" Mother hisses vehemently, poking me in the small of my back to hurry me along.

The inside of the chapel is adorned with simple white and dark green ribbons, with floral arrangements flanking the marital podium. The priest is already standing there waiting. I have known him since childhood. His name is Father Harrison and I spent much of my younger years wanting to marry *him*, actually. He is an older man, but to a young girl like me, he was the pinnacle of manly ideal. He has been the head of our congregation ever since I can remember, leading the services with a loud, powerful voice and elaborate gestures.

Now, of course, he is old and grey, but still charismatic. When his eyes land on me, he holds his arms open in a stance of welcome. "Little Cassandra Meadows! Hard to believe that it's time for you to become a real woman of God!"

His warm smile reassures me, even as my father's hand on my shoulder must be leaving a bruise. Daddy waves to him as he rushes me into a tiny side room to await the ceremony. My mother stands in the dark chamber with me, the both of us quietly listening to the crowds filing into the chapel pews. I peer through a crack in the door, the sliver of space allowing me a very limited view of the church interior. I see my fiancé walk briskly down the aisle, his back straight and head held tall. I can't see any details, but just the sight of his hulking frame is enough to send a shiver down my spine. I feel so small and fragile in contrast to him.

Everyone is tittering excitedly, quietly, as he passes down the aisle. I blush, knowing that my fellow churchgoers are confused by the fact that nobody recognizes him. He is something very rare, indeed: a stranger in our midst. Surely, they must all be questioning how he managed to sneak his way in. I can just imagine the whispers going around, *"Who is this strange man?" "Is he one of us?"*

And the worst of all: *"How in the world did they ever even meet?"*

I want to vomit, right here in the side chamber of my own wedding chapel. My mother seems to pick up on my nerves, as she gently brushes the hair off of my shoulder and kisses the side of my head.

"Don't be afraid, dear. I know it is daunting, but we all must take this vow. Trust in God to protect you," she says, so softly I can barely hear her.

"I want to make you and Daddy proud, but I'm scared," I reply, in an equally low voice.

"We *are* proud, Cassie. Just be strong."

Outside in the church, the crowds are all cooing

"aww" and I look through the crack to see my little brother, tiny, sweet Isaiah, walking down the aisle holding what looks like a ring pillow. His unruly brown hair is swept back using a copious amount of gel, and there is a half-frightened, half-petulant look on his cherubic face. My heart surges in my chest, and I have the sudden urge to burst out of the chamber, rush down the aisle, and scoop him up in my arms. Something deep in my soul tells me that I won't be seeing him very often after today.

I miss him already.

Fighting back tears for the millionth time today, I straighten my shoulders and try to look radiantly happy as my mother opens the chamber door and pushes me out. My father is waiting nearby to take my arm and lead me down the aisle.

Everyone swivels in their pews, all eyes falling on me. I feel nauseous, gulping back a sob as Daddy smiles down at me and begins to walk me down the aisle to my fiancé, standing at the end of the walkway. The stranger is tall and imposing, towering over everyone, even Father Harrison.

The same dizziness that shook me before threatens to take me down now. My father senses my weakness and braces himself, subtly leaning into me as we approach the front of the church. My heart is galloping in my rib cage, beating so fast and so loudly that I wonder how nobody has noticed it yet. Finally, we are there. I'm standing at the marital podium next to my daddy and Father Harrison, looking up at...

My new husband.

He is just as scary as I remembered in my hazy memories of the other night. He is startlingly handsome. Frighteningly good-looking. He has hawklike, watchful dark eyes, a long, straight nose, sensuous lips, and cropped black hair. His cheekbones are so high and sharp I think they could cut glass. And of course, even his fitted, immaculately-tailored black suit cannot hide his bulging muscles. I glance between Daddy, Father Harrison, and my fiancé — the latter is by far the biggest one.

I am so caught up in cataloguing the gorgeous, terrifying features of my future husband that I totally zone out during the ceremony! Father Harrison is droning on and on about the duties of a Godly woman to her husband, explaining what I already know from years of education: that my sole purpose in life is to serve my father... and then my husband.

"Do you, Cassandra Bethany Meadows, take Andrei Abramovich Petrov to be your lawfully wedded husband, to love and to serve as ordained by our formidable God?" Father Harrison asks of me, taking my hand and lifting it up.

I am shaken by the sudden realization that this is the first time I've heard his name. Then it hits me that I have to respond.

"Y-yes. I do," I say quickly, my voice sounding a little thin.

"And do you, Andrei Abramovich Petrov, take Cassandra Bethany Meadows to be your lawfully wedded wife, to guide and to protect as ordained by our formidable God?"

Andrei, my new husband, looks at me deep in the eyes. I feel a sharp stab to my gut as though his gaze is physically piercing my body. I try not to flinch.

In a deep, velvety voice, he replies: "I do."

"*Y*ou may now kiss the bride."

I can practically feel her heart beating furiously through the palms of her hands as we hear those words, and she looks up at me with wide, anxious eyes. She puts on a strong show for these people, and I'm impressed by how well she's kept herself together all this time.

Most women envision their wedding day to be the most magical moment of their lives, but I can only imagine the fear in her heart before my looming figure. She must feel alone and backed into a corner, her parents selling her off like a commodity, the rest of her cold family expecting her to perform like a doll today, and I just know she looks at me and sees me for the criminal I am.

But through it all, she looks angelic. Where she looked exposed and vulnerable up on the auction stage, she looks now like she should be in her element — a heavenly figure clothed in an immaculate dress.

After a brief pause, she offers a shy smile, fear still written in her eyes, and we lean into each other, our lips pressing together.

It's a chaste kiss, but I feel her draw breath as she's pressed up against my face, and her hands tighten in my grip as she feels the warmth of my mouth. Is this really her first kiss?

We break after only a moment, the poor girl too dazed by the whole ceremony and the rush of what's happening to her to savor the moment. Even as I give her hand a squeeze, she blinks and looks confused, but not displeased as the audience begins to clap for us and the organ wedding music starts up.

"Brothers and sisters of the church, Mr. and Mrs. Petrov."

A few moments later, we're walking down the aisle towards the door, the rest of Cassie's relatives smiling and bobbing their heads at us, many of them in poorly-fitted suits and reeking from an overuse of perfume. Many of their faces are stony even as they clap, as if this were a grave ritual rather than a cause for celebration. It's all too familiar to me, though I can't quite place why.

I feel like I'm guiding my shaky bride through the underworld as we pass through all these people she seems to know only tangentially. I see a lot of simple colors all around — the wedding was obviously thrown together at the last minute, but for that, I can't blame anyone but Cassie's parents.

We come out the doors of the chapel as man and wife, a Bratva assassin and his wife who's never so much as spent time alone in a room with a man. As we're ushered into the reception shortly after, that much and more becomes clear to me.

THE RECEPTION HALL is a wide room dotted with round tables, and after an arduously long prayer session in which everyone in the room was asked to link hands and bow their heads, the rest of the guests begin to eat while Cassie and I sit side by side at the table in the center of the room, where we're victims of all the passing-by relatives.

A number of them stop by to try to make conversation with me, but while Cassie is seated quietly to my left, her parents have taken up posts to my right, fielding most of the prying relatives' questions.

"So, are you a friend from Cassie's home church?" an older man with patchy, white hair inquires. The term itself is foreign to me.

"No," Arnold Meadows, Cassie's father, interjects. "He and Cassie met over business, actually. Andrei's father is an entrepreneur, you know, very well-traveled man, self-made. Never able to stay put anywhere, so the poor man couldn't make it, but Andrei's been handling the business on his behalf here in the States, and well," Arnold pats me on the back as if I were a nephew or something, "he just fit right into the family!"

The old man seems satisfied, and he and Arnold chat a while as I peer around at the rest of the room, only half paying attention. The lies that roll off her father's tongue are easy and practiced, like someone who has been lying his entire life. He very likely has, to get to the point where he's willing to sell off his own child to a stranger at *that* auction.

I hear the family chattering about who knows who from where, what "denomination" this part of the family has defected to, who's acted wrongly against whom in the family, and so on. It all sounds remarkably like the kinds of things the Bratva discusses at big, informal meetings, I realize. This whole ceremony has felt a lot like that, with just as many falsehoods being spun.

There was nothing like this back home in Siberia. As a boy growing up in an orphanage, I remember very little interaction with the Orthodox Church, and I rarely heard anything about it. It was simply outside my sphere of life, and as I grew into a man who had to do what he had to to get by, it was almost out of my mind entirely.

Being surrounded by a group of people whose entire life is clearly oriented around this institution is strange, but not incomprehensible. This is all clearly about relations, and as a man nearly bound to the Bratva, it isn't too unfamiliar.

But this isn't even like the Churches I know of here in the States. There's an air of secrecy and deception thick in the air, not just from her father, but from the others as well. They all ask questions expecting a coded lie, and respond in kind.

I turn to my bride, and I find her picking at her food uncomfortably.

"Do you like it?" I ask, and she jumps a little, enraptured in her own world.

"Oh, yes, it's...it's good. I think one of my aunts made most of the food."

An awkward pause lingers between us. I can only imagine the fear that's binding her, but just as Oskar had promised, she seems intent on pleasing me and all the people around us. I clear my throat before swiftly changing the subject. "So, you know most of these people well, yes?"

Cassie shifts in her seat and looks around, pursing her lips. "Kind of."

I wait for her to say more, but nothing else comes. She only looks at me for a moment as if she too were waiting for me to say more, but she averts her eyes and takes a drink after half a moment. She's still shaken up. I can't blame her, after everything she's been through in the past few days.

Arnold's voice catches my ear again, and I glance over at him, catching part of his conversation.

"Oh no doubt," he's saying to another man about his age, "a young girl her age can't be going out to dances like that so late, that's a ticket to trouble. I'll bring it up at the next PTA meeting, and I'll be praying for her in the meantime, brother."

"You know, I said the same thing to her youth pastor, but these young people just can't keep their hands off each other, even with chaperones," the other man says, and I tune out of the conversation, figuring it's going to go on like this for a while.

I realize I have a level of growing contempt for Cassie's father. Arnold reminds me of Sergei in too many ways. He's all smiles around other men who hold the same power as he, but when it comes to handling himself in private, I can smell the brute of a man he really is.

Every now and then, Cassie's mother Jan tries to get a word in edgewise in the conversation, but Arnold is quick to interrupt her. After some time, I notice her resignation and how she keeps her eyes on her food.

I wonder how monstrously he must treat his wife and daughter at home. A man who would be willing to sell his daughter into debt must be twisted beyond comprehension to be able to sleep at night.

As the two men drone on in their conversation, I hear Arnold repeating a point Jan had made almost verbatim. Feeling exhausted just by being in the proximity, I speak up.

"Jan said that a moment ago."

The two men stop at my sudden interjection, and Arnold raises an eyebrow. "Pardon?"

"What you just said about your church's youth program providing women's social groups — Jan brought that up a few minutes ago before you interrupted her."

Arnold starts to go red, while the middle-aged man speaking to him clears his throat. "R-right, must have missed that. Anyhow, I'll see you around, Arnie. Enjoy the food."

He and Arnold exchange a nod, and before he turns back to his food, Arnold glares daggers at me while Jan pretends she hasn't heard any part of the exchange, her cheeks bright. I can't help but smile a little at the man's embarrassment, and I dig back into my food with a little more vigor.

Cassie is paralyzed by the subtle exchange. I imagine that challenges to her father's authority must not be common in the household.

I know already that Arnold won't like me. Even if I wanted to be cozy with that *govnosos*, I'm an outsider here in every respect. I can feel it in the way everyone here regards me. This is a tight-knit community already, but as a Russian who knows nobody, this cold, cordial kindness is the best they'll be willing to muster.

The rest of the dinner goes uneventfully, and after dinner, the time comes for me to drive my bride back to my home in Brighton Beach.

The family gives us both stiff goodbyes, and I exchange names with and receive business cards from a staggering amount of people I have no intention of seeing ever again. I can tell they hope the same, even as they keep up appearances.

There's a certain finality to the goodbyes Cassie exchanges with her closer relatives, a few cousins who she might have known better than others. I'm reminded of what a foreigner I am to these people, and I realize that this ceremony is cutting Cassie off from these people altogether. She seems most upset about her brother, who'd fallen asleep earlier in the evening, but whom she went to kiss goodbye anyways, after asking my permission.

She's being given to me, and in this community, the husband dictates how the new family will be run — where we go, what we do, and how we behave. In marrying Cassie off to someone like me, she's getting sent away for good, and many of the family sense it, but none dare question it.

I can't decide if it's for better or for worse for her.

But then I see her father embracing her, hugging her tight to him, but there's no love in the embrace. His eyes meet mine for a moment as he hugs her, and I realize this man is little better than a jealous ape giving away what he sees as one of his possessions. Cassie's tearful embrace with her mother is the only one of the night that seems to have some emotion to it.

Finally, we're walking out the doors for the last time, her hand in mine as I guide her to my car, a sleek black corvette I keep for special occasions. I didn't let anyone decorate it for the event.

Rice is thrown at us as we make our way down, and a few times, I feel Cassie's legs start to wobble as she loses her balance.

We finally reach my car, and I hold the door open for her, helping her into the sleek leather seats, tucking all of her long white gown in before shutting the door.

A moment later, I get in on the driver's side, and we pull away, leaving those strange people behind us as we drive south.

Once we're a ways down the road from the church, I feel like I should say something, to try to make small talk about the big night, how she must feel in all the rush, or something along those lines, but I can't bring myself to see such words as anything more than cruel and unnecessary. So we sit in silence.

I glance over at Cassie as we get onto the highway. She's looking out the window, her expression unreadable, but now that she's far away from the claws of her family, her beauty seems to jump out at me all the more.

Against the cold black color of the car's interior, Cassie couldn't contrast more. Her white wedding dress, blonde hair, pale skin, and blue eyes that sparkle in the setting sun make her look like a diamond beside me.

A feeling of satisfaction rises in my chest as I look back to the road. Cassie is the most pristine woman I've ever laid eyes on, and I'm taking her away from a group of people unworthy of her. The world is cruel to women like her, and she's been dealt an even more oppressive hand.

The least I can do is protect her from everything else she'll have to face, living with a man like me.

As we drive the three-hour trip to Brighton Beach, I notice Cassie nodding off to sleep in the silence. I personally enjoy the quiet the trip affords, being used to the city noise and the thrum of clubs as I do my work, and I hope Cassie can take some solace in gathering her thoughts in relative privacy.

But the thought of what will happen when we reach my apartment keeps coming back to me. Cassie has curled up into the seat, sleeping gracefully with her arms wrapped around herself as she dozes.

I can't deny that I desire her. Even as my impulse was to protect her, I desire her. But I know she expects me to take her as my property, to use her however I please the moment we step into the bedroom. With such an upbringing, it's doubtful she was even told that she has the ability to say 'no' to such things.

So what will she think when we reach my home — our home? I think for a wild moment that I could just give her some money and send her on her own way, to be independent, but I realize that would only send her back home. She doesn't know how to take care of herself out there.

I will have to be her protector, no matter what she desires.

Somehow, I feel a hint of warmth at the idea in my heart. I don't know what her desires will be when we cross our marriage threshold, but that doesn't change the fact that this lovely young woman is my responsibility, regardless of how I'd like to claim her as mine with all the hot-blooded passion she's been able to stir up in my heart in such a short time.

What have I gotten myself into?

# CASSIE

The moon is high in the velvety black sky when I am gently prodded awake. At first, I am confused and disoriented, thinking that I must still be in my bed at home. Is it really six o'clock already? I have to hurry downstairs to start making eggs and sausage for Daddy and Isaiah, my mother must be annoyed with me for oversleeping...

I sit up with a jolt when it dawns on me where I actually am: the passenger seat of my new husband's luxurious Corvette. I blink my bleary eyes rapidly, taking in my chrome and leather surroundings, my puffy white dress, my hair starting to fray loose from my French braid. There's a hand on my shoulder, and for once it isn't my father's. It's lighter, gentler, yet it still feels commanding. Maybe even more so, since it won't leave a harsh bruise beneath my pale skin.

My eyes follow the hand up the arm to the broad shoulder of Andrei Petrov, the man I am now married to, forevermore, for better or for worse. I bite my lip and avert my gaze demurely, suddenly ashamed. I can't believe I fell asleep in the car. On my wedding night. My father would be furious with me for being so rude.

"Sorry to wake you," he says gruffly, a faint Russian accent sneaking through.

I shake my head and offer a weak smile, trying to remember that I must be a perfect wife and partner. I must be docile and sweet and pretty. No matter how frightened I am, it is of the utmost importance that I maintain my willing, humble service to my husband.

It's what God intends for me.

"No, no, I am sorry for falling asleep. Couldn't have been great conversation on the ride here, with me unconscious," I reply, tucking my hair behind my ear.

"I'm glad you were able to get some rest. You may need it."

My heart skips at his words. I suddenly feel very warm and tingly, a strange sensation tickling between my thighs. Curiosity tinged with fear works its way through my body. I don't quite know exactly what he means, but I have an inkling that it might not be very wholesome.

Andrei gets out of the car and rushes to open my

door before I even get the chance to reach for the lever. He offers a big, calloused hand and after a second's hesitation, I gingerly place my tiny hand in his. The rough texture of his fingers wrapped around my smooth, pale hand sends a tremble down my back. He gently pulls me up out of the Corvette and guides me to the sidewalk. Looking around, it hits me that we are in the city.

Staring up at the massive brick building in front of us, I stammer, "Is th-this really where you live?" I can hear distant sirens and horns honking, even though it's the middle of the night. Back home, everything is silent at night. In fact, even during the day I rarely ever heard anything but chirping birds and the sounds of children playing outside.

"Yes. I imagine it will be an adjustment for you," Andrei replies simply.

I turn to look at him, more than a little fearful. "I've never been to the city before."

He raises both eyebrows in genuine surprise as he holds open the lobby door for me and I walk through into a beautifully furnished lobby, with dark wood paneling and sleek black chairs and couches. "You've really never seen the city before?"

I shake my head, feeling a blush creep into my cheeks. "I have never left my hometown. Except... that one time of course," I say, feeling the embarrassment grow. He of course knows what time I mean.

"Not even for a day?"

Is it really so hard to believe? I'm beginning to feel a little attacked. After all, there was never really any good reason to leave town. My city is small and insular, of course, but it's always had everything we needed. I wonder if my new husband is some kind of jet-setter.

"Not once," I answer.

"How sad," Andrei says, leading me to the elevator.

I dare not tell him that I've never been in an elevator before; I only know what they are from what I've seen in books. When the metal doors shut together, the two of us are left standing in a tiny, cramped chamber with mirrored walls. I can't avoid looking at our reflections. We are surrounded by them. When it moves, my legs quiver, and he holds me a little tighter against his hard body, keeping me standing.

It strikes me now just how drastically different we are in every way. Andrei is frighteningly tall and muscular, and everything about him is cold and dark. He towers over my diminutive frame, and his dark eyes and black hair contrast sharply with my pale blonde hair and light blue eyes. We are night and day, the two of us.

I wonder to myself what will happen now that we are joined together.

What happens when the night meets the day? When the moon touches the sun?

An eclipse?

We ride the elevator all the way up to the ninth floor, and I cannot believe I'm even *inside* a building with so many floors, much less going to live in one. We step out into a hallway with hardwood floors and walk down a ways to a door labeled 905.

"Is this one yours?" I ask, looking up at Andrei.

Without missing a beat, he answers, "It is ours."

My stomach does a flip flop and I gulp hard as the tall, powerful man beside me unlocks the door to my new home. My mouth falls open the second I step inside.

It's the most beautiful place I've ever been, with high ceilings and massive, wide windows along the stark white walls. The foyer opens directly into a huge, airy living room area, with the shiny, high-tech kitchen to the left and two doors leading to what I assume are a bathroom and bedroom on the right. The floors are made of a glossy, nearly black wood, and the furnishings are all variations of black and white. A small spiral staircase in the corner of the room leads up to what appears to be a sort of loft area. Crossing the room to stand in front of the windows, I draw back the heavy black curtains and gasp at the sight of the New York City skyline, an array of sparkling lights speckled in the pitch-black night like constellations.

Suddenly, I tremble at the touch of a hand falling at my waist. I swivel around to face my new husband, who is looking down at me with a tight-jawed expression. There's something vaguely predatory flickering in his deep, dark eyes, and I inhale sharply as he raises my hand to kiss it with his full lips. Apart from my father, I have never felt a man's lips on my skin before. In my dazed state at the wedding, I hardly perceived our first sanctioned kiss as husband and wife. My head was so fuzzy and filled with racing thoughts that it had simply passed me by. But now, alone in this apartment with the city teeming with nocturnal life, the sensation is startlingly pleasant, and I almost want to recoil from it. After all, pleasure is forbidden, and especially when it's *this* kind of pleasure.

"Do you like it?" Andrei asks, and at first I think he's talking about the kiss. Then I realize that he wants to know if I like the apartment. And I do, very much.

"Y-yes," I reply, perhaps a little too quickly. "It's beautiful."

"I know the furnishings may be a little too simple to suit a feminine taste," he admits, and he is partially correct. The apartment is utterly gorgeous, but it is a very minimalistic kind of beauty. The few items he does have are obviously of a very high quality, but he doesn't have much more than the essentials. There is one black couch and one white chair. One massive flat-screen television mounted on the wall. Everything is monochrome and cold, very cold.

It's the sort of aesthetic that reminds me of snow-capped mountains: breathtaking to behold but not particularly hospitable in practice.

"If you'd like, perhaps you could lend some of your warmth to the place," Andrei added, brushing the hair back from my face and peering into my eyes as though searching for... something.

I instinctively flinch from his touch, and I see a shadow of regret cross his features. I immediately feel awful, as though I must do something to make amends.

I *must* be a perfect wife. It is my purpose in life to serve.

"Whatever you want from me is yours," I reply diplomatically, giving him a smile.

His expression shifts into one that frightens me; he looks like a wolf about to devour his prey — and I am the unfortunate little white rabbit. My heart starts to pound rapidly in my chest and I back up ever so slightly, the coolness of the windowpane raising goosebumps up my spine. Andrei steps forward, coming closer to me, effectively pinning me between his huge body and the NYC backdrop. I draw a sharp intake of breath when he pushes up against me, his thick frame oppressive and imposing.

"In that case, I will tell you what I want..." he growls, leaning down so that his rugged profile is only mere inches from my own face. My heart is racing so fast I worry it might explode. Tracing my jawline with one long finger, he whispers, "I want *you.*"

And with that, he swoops in to press his lips against mine, and my breath catches in my throat as my whole body stiffens. His hand comes around to cup the back of my head and his tongue pushes gently into my mouth, a sensation I have never even dreamed of before.

"Andrei," I gasp when he releases me for a moment. My mind is racing and I can't manage to pin a single coherent thought in place. I can feel some strange, foreign warmth spreading from the forbidden space between my legs. His hand drops down to grope my backside, hard. I let out a soft squeal, feeling my cheeks burn bright pink. What is he doing? How is he making me feel this way? This cannot be what God intends.

"*Chyort*, you are so beautiful," he says, his voice gravelly and low.

"I — I don't know wh-what to do," I stammer softly, searching his handsome face for some kind of reasonable answer. I don't understand what I should be doing with my hands, my lips. And should I really feel this good?

My entire body is surging with heat and — dare I admit it? — desire.

"Shh, *malyshka*, you don't have to do anything. Let me take control."

Before I can utter another syllable, his lips are on

mine again, more forcefully this time. His hands rove up and down my body, squeezing my backside, my hips, and sliding up to cup my breasts. Part of me wants to revolt against this sinful assault and push his hands away, break away down to the street and run all the way home to my quiet town, back to my routine and my closed-off life. But the devil himself must have worked his way into my bones, because I find myself totally powerless, limp and pliable in the arms of this hulking, dangerous man.

And what's more, I am even enjoying it.

When he dives forward to graze his teeth along my neck, I can't suppress a surprised moan falling from my lips. I tremble at his touch, the drag of his teeth and suckling of his lips bordering on slightly painful to my tingling skin. But I don't pull away, even when he brushes the hair off of my shoulder and slides the sleeve of my wedding dress down to reveal more of my collarbone. He plants a trail of hard, nipping kisses along my throat and chest, my breath quickening as his lips move downward toward my heaving breasts. I am not ample-bosomed by any means, as my frame is more slender and slight, but Andrei seems hungry for my flesh.

I want to whisper no, to protest this blatant sin, but I can't find the words.

He hastily unlaces my wedding dress and pushes it down, the sudden onslaught of cool air on my exposed skin making me gasp. I am now clad only in a simple white lace bra and matching panties, and garters on my trembling thighs. Andrei lets out a raspy groan at the sight of me and I feel myself growing damp between my legs, to my dismay. I know, logically, that he has already seen me nearly naked before, in that horrible, dank basement. But this? This is completely different. It's just the two of us, and I am not being paraded for sale.

I've already been bought.

I belong to this man completely and utterly, and my body is his possession.

So I don't stop him when he unhooks my bra and tosses it aside, my nipples standing erect in the cool air. Andrei cups my breasts and drags his tongue across my right nipple, causing me to cry out with an unexpected jolt of pleasure. All of this is so foreign to me; I have never even touched my own body in this way before, as it is a terrible sin to do so.

But it feels more heavenly than sinful, the way his lips and fingertips caress and tease my breasts, nipping and fondling me until I cry out and clutch at his back, trying desperately to draw him ever closer to me. I've never felt like this before, and even though I know deep down that this is the devil's work, I can't help longing for more.

"Ohh, Andrei," I breathe, my eyes rolling back in my head. He grunts his appreciation, his mouth trailing down my taut stomach in a ticklish path of kisses. When he reaches my panties, I hold my breath unintentionally, waiting to see what he does next.

I glance down at him to see his dark eyes fixed on my face, as though expecting some kind of signal. I know I should tell him to stop. But I can't bring myself to do that.

"Please... more," I manage to squeak out.

That is all he needs to hear before tearing my panties down my legs and spreading my thighs apart. I am panting with need when he does the unthinkable: he presses his tongue against my warm, wet folds, sending a shockwave of pleasure through my body. My hips jut forward instinctively, my body shuddering as he relentlessly sucks and licks between my legs.

A half-strangled cry bursts from my throat as I feel the tension mounting deep inside me. Tears moisten my eyes and my hands grapple to brace myself against the window. Somewhere, distantly, in the back of my mind, a voice is screaming at me that my naked body is pressed up against a window for all the residents of New York City to see, reminding me that I should feel ashamed of the position I'm currently in. But that voice is drowned out by the overwhelming, pounding rhythm of my heartbeat and the involuntary rolling of my hips against Andrei's glorious, warm mouth.

Until I suddenly remember that this, all of this, is a horrible sin. My ingrained shame comes barreling out of the darkness to hit me so hard I see stars, my body drawing back instinctively. I can't allow myself to enjoy something like this! It's obscene! It's unholy!

I open my mouth to beg Andrei to stop, but before I get the chance, he senses me pulling away and wraps his arms around my legs to drag me back, a little too forcefully. He groans into my pulsing, slick flower with a wild hunger, plunging his tongue inside me and suckling that tight, mind-numbing little bud of nerves until I feel myself getting closer and closer to...

"Ohh! Andrei!" I cry out as a powerful wave of ecstasy rushes through me, radiating ripples of pleasure outward from between my legs. I shudder and my knees buckle, my body going limp from the overwhelming sensation, but Andrei grabs me and holds me up in place, refusing to release me. His mouth devours me ravenously, mercilessly, licking up the flow of honey with abandon. The overstimulation is enough to make me feel dizzy, like I might faint any moment. It feels so good, even though his relentless manipulations linger on the verge of painful.

To my surprise, another climax crashes through me and this time I can't stop myself from squealing and collapsing into Andrei's waiting arms, utterly exhausted. He carries me easily, as though I'm nothing but a bouquet of flowers in his arms. Through my spinning, hazy vision I can see us walking through a door into the bedroom. Andrei cradles me gently onto the bed, my tired limbs sinking thankfully into the plush sheets.

The last thing I remember is the feeling of his lips gently kissing my forehead and his soft, low growl: "Welcome home."

## ANDREI

*I* smooth her hair as I watch her start to drift off to sleep, and I lie there beside her for a while, watching her practically glow. I watch her chest rise and fall, and within a few minutes, the rhythm becomes slow, steady, and peaceful, the bliss of her first time written on her smiling face as she snuggles into the blankets.

Quietly, I roll out of bed and make my way out of the bedroom, careful not to wake Cassie as I creep to the walk-in closet adjacent to the master bedroom. As satisfying as this night has been, it is not yet over with.

I have a job tonight, and specifically, a ballet to attend.

I have my suit for tonight pressed and hanging in plain sight in the closet, along with a pair of shoes and white gloves. All nice, but not too nice —

certainly nothing I'd wear out to a public appearance, but tonight is a special circumstance. I slip the whole outfit on in a matter of seconds, quiet as a shadow. I've become skilled at changing my clothes quickly and quietly. Jeans and a leather jacket might be my usual duds, but they won't get me into a high-class performance in Manhattan.

Before I leave, I stick my head into the room to look at Cassie one more time. She's laying on her side now, curling up around one of the pillows on the bed, a smile still written across her face. I see my shadow cast over her from the faint light behind me, and before long, I close the door and step away.

On my way out, I grab a small briefcase containing my only two tools for the evening: a thin metal wire and a valuable bottle of Pétrus wine, straight from Bordeaux.

A few moments later, I'm out the back door and pulling out of the driveway, silent as night. My car makes its way through the inky-black streets of NYC towards Manhattan.

Ordinarily, I wouldn't have agreed to take any work on my wedding night, impromptu as this one was, but the hit that I'm to execute tonight is something of a personal matter.

Back when I was growing up, the city streets in Yakutsk offered very little comfort to homeless teenagers in the dead of winter. Not long before I found myself in the care of the Bratva, I found myself facing certain death under just those circumstances. More than a few boys had frozen to death out there, and that night, I was sure I was going to be one of them.

A kindly woman took pity on me. Her name was Mariya, and she had a child daughter named Sonya. Mariya gave me food and shelter for the night, and the next day, she sent me to find a man who she said would take care of me, give me a future — that man turned out to be a friend of the Bratva, and my career began there.

But I did not forget Mariya and her little Sonya. I stayed in touch, and she would write me endless letters about her beloved daughter. Sonya was a talented dancer; even though Mariya was a food peddler with little money when I met her, she prospered and saved enough to move to Moscow, eventually putting her daughter into ballet.

Sonya must have been rather talented indeed, because I learned that before long, she was discovered by one Jean Bouchard, a world-famous ballet coach on tour there. He offered to take little Sonya, then nine years old, under his wing, dancing across Europe and America to live out her dreams.

This offer was a dream come true for the both of them, and they readily accepted. For a long time, until very recently, all I knew of Sonya was that she was sending money back home, and that she seemed very happy.

Then I received a more urgent, discrete message from Mariya.

It had been two years since she had heard from her daughter. Two years of silence after regular contact. The money was still coming, but never a word. She started asking questions, probing friends of friends for information about her daughter, now seventeen years old.

It reached her through the grapevine that Sonya's dream had become a nightmare.

Ever since taking her from home, Jean had been monstrous to her. The training regimen for a ballerina already pushes the boundaries of what is healthy for the human body, but Jean pushed Sonya many times harder. Jean controlled everything Sonya did; what she ate, when and how she slept, how she breathed, carried herself in public, spoke. She had no friends — she knew only her training.

As Sonya got older, it only got worse. Jean had hospital bills quietly covered up, hiding traces of his prized dancer's malnutrition. When she was fifteen, he's started her on drugs to keep her lively and active for her non-stop training and increasingly prestigious performances.

I did some research of my own on Jean, and this all seemed to be in the routine for him. More than one of his previous protégés had ended their careers broken, sick, or worse, and there were rumors that

Jean could get too personal for comfort with his trainees.

Mariya was heartbroken to learn all this, but her sorrow was only matched by her fury. When she reached out to me, she sent me every last kopeck of the money Sonya had been sending her. It was all of her savings. She wanted Jean to pay for this.

In truth, the money was but a fraction of what such a high-profile target was worth, but to this woman, I owed my life.

And I would pay her with someone else's.

I pull up at the Metropolitan Opera House as droves of people in expensive attire were filing in, laughing and chattering to each other. I make my way around all of them, heading for one of the employee entrances. I won't be questioned thoroughly until I hit a checkpoint — I'm dressed in the exact outfit as the serving staff.

Before getting out of my car, I tuck the wire into my coat pocket and take out the bottle of wine. I had to have it in place just before the start of the performance.

As I approach the entrance, a guard nods to me as I flash my fake ID badge. Workers come in and out constantly, so it's rare that a security guard at a place like this can spot a new face with any certainty. If anything, I'm just another late server.

I keep the bottle of wine low at my side, not

conspicuously being hidden, but not in plain sight either.

The crowd is bustling by the time I make it to the hallways. I know the staff routes well enough by now — I've had plenty of time to research this place. Ordinarily, I would be loath to perform a hit at such a public venue as this, but Mariya was very clear in her instructions; Jean has been pushing Sonya to the brink of death for tonight's performance, and she wants to return the favor. She wants him to know why this is happening.

Yet even as I try to stay focused on my objective, as I see the droves of beautiful, wealthy people milling about busily, many of them glowing with laughter and anticipation for the show, I can't help but think back to the way Cassie looked on my bed, pristine in the dim light.

As I gently push past a number of other servers on my way to the private boxes, the strangest thoughts plague my mind. I feel like I'd enjoy taking Cassie to a place like this — not a hit, but to a classy show, a taste of the New York culture she's been deprived of all her life.

I have to push the thoughts away as I approach my target's location.

Jean Bouchard enjoys watching the fruits of his work as much as he enjoys tormenting his dancers. Rather than spending the performance behind the stage, he prefers to watch from one of the most expensive boxes in the theater. As I approached the box, I flashed my ID card once again for the guard posted at the door, who nods at me after seeing me hold up my bottle of wine significantly.

"Best hurry, you won't be able to get in after curtain," the guard warns, and I bob my head in acknowledgement, preferring not to speak if I can avoid it.

I step in and see Jean chatting with a couple of wealthy-looking women seated on either side of him. Jean is a thin man of towering height, with a shaven face and bald head that accentuates his already intense black eyebrows. An alien-looking figure, to be sure, but there's an eerie cruelty to his smile as he fakes a laugh at someone's joke that reminds me what kind of man I'm dealing with.

"Monsieur Bouchard," I politely interrupt them, and the world-famous coach arches an eyebrow and gives me a vaguely annoyed look. I hold up the wine and address him in his native French, with an accent I've rehearsed a thousand times. "Complements of the theater, a bottle of Pétrus, for your enjoyment. We're honored to have you this evening."

At the sound of his language, his expression eases a bit, and he manages something like a sincere smile as he replies in kind. "I see. Return my compliments. You are dismissed." He waves me off without a tip, and I bow my head politely, retreating out the door.

All I need do now is wait.

I step out the doors and make my way to the vicinity of the closest bathroom. The Bordeaux wine is authentic, and it's a favorite of Jean's, but I treated it with a potent, tasteless diuretic before resealing and delivering it. In a place like this, at a performance, I have very slim chances of getting Jean alone. During a performance like this, however, it's more unlikely that the guests will be taking frequent bathroom breaks, so the restrooms should be relatively empty.

And as much as Jean will want to watch his star pupil on stage, he won't have much choice but to answer the call of nature.

Within a few minutes, the music starts, and as I stand by one of the doorways to the regular rows, I can see the performers begin the show.

It's *Swan Lake*. I chuckle to myself. A fine Russian ballet was appropriate for a job like this. As the ballet gets underway, my eyes are torn between watching for my target and watching the stage.

Before long, I see Sonya, bounding across the stage with the grace of a deer. It's remarkable to see how she's grown — she was a tiny child when I saw her last. Then again, I was but a teenager at the time.

Her movements are effortless, as if the music is at her command rather than the other way around. Through it all, I can see something missing from her expression. There's a tinge of emotionlessness in her eyes, a lack of the fire I saw in her when she was younger.

As I watch her carry out a flawless performance in sadness, my mind wanders again back to Cassie, thinking about her background. Cassie has all the grace in the world, all the beauty of an angel, and all the innocence of a lamb, but how many times did I see her looking to be on the verge of tears at her own wedding? How much did her parents put her through before she ended up on that auction stage?

Cassie tasted so sweet, and I know the lust within me craves, demands to have my face between her thighs again and again. I wanted to ruin that perfect angel, but I can't shake the thought of how much of her personhood was taken from her to make her what she is, just like Sonya.

Footsteps down the hall snap me out of my trance, and I realize, embarrassed, that I'd let nearly an hour pass watching the show. Out of the corner of my eye, I spot Jean's form disappearing into the bathroom.

Without missing another beat, I start off after him.

The bathroom is long and luxurious, with mirrors all along the wall with the sinks. The lone sound of urination tells me that I'm fortunate enough to be alone with Jean. Quietly, I slip out my wire and keep it tight in one hand, moving to one of the sink mirrors to pretend to be adjusting my collar.

Jean finishes relieving himself and goes to wash his hands, the water creating some white noise in the long bathroom. As he does, I see him glance over at me.

"Fine wine," he remarks curtly, "a rare thing in this country."

"Very," I reply, chuckling lightly and stepping in his direction as if headed to the urinal myself, "rare as a talented young dancer from Yakutsk."

In the mirror, I see Jean's brow furrow as he digests what I've said, and in half a breath, I bring the garroting wire around his neck and yank back tight.

"I have a message from a loving mother," I growl into his ear in my lightly accented English as the wire digs into the skin of his neck, and I see him try to shout something as he watches his face turning purple in the mirror, arms flailing uselessly.

I pull the wire tighter around his neck much harder than usual as the thought of Cassie in Sonya's place flashes into my mind. Jean's body is lithe, but he's out of practice. I was expecting more of a fight from him, and after only a short time, I feel his body go limp, eyes rolling up into the back of his head as I let him gently to the ground on the bathroom floor.

With white-gloved hands, I drag the strangled man to the handicap bathroom stall and set him up

SOLD TO THE HITMAN

on the toilet. That should buy me all the time I need to slip out of the building. I lock the door on the inside and crawl out under the door.

I adjust my tie, checking myself over for blood in the mirror. I'm clean. There's always a certain weight off my shoulders just after the job is complete. After that point, all I need to worry about is the getaway. After checking over the sinks for stray hairs I might have dropped, I start to head for the bathroom door.

Then I hear a sound that makes my blood curdle.

A choked voice croaks something out in French from the bathroom door. "Brother...murder... the Russians..."

As soon as I hear the voice, I sprint back to the stall, sliding under the door with practiced dexterity, my heart pounding a thousand beats a minute.

To my horror, Jean is holding a cell phone to his ear, his face still swollen and blood trickling out his mouth as he gets a message out, bloodshot eyes staring straight into me.

Springing to my feet, I deliver a swift strike to his neck that ends the last sliver of life in his cold heart, and the phone clatters to the ground.

I hear a voice crying something from the other line in alarm. *"Jean?! Jean! What's happening?"* Before another word comes out, I crush the phone under my heel.

*Shit.*

I crouch down and put my fingers to Jean's neck, checking his pulse. Nothing. Crawling out from under the stall again, I make my way out the door and take a walk that feels far longer than it is down the stairs and out the doors of the Metropolitan Opera House, knowing that every second I lingered now put me closer to being caught.

* * *

SOME TIME LATER, I'm back at my apartment, slipping in as quietly as I exited.

My heart calmed itself long ago; I'd had to learn to become adept at maintaining composure even in the midst of disasters like that. But while I manage to keep panic away, the fury I feel at myself for making such a slip-up is unmitigated.

*One more second, and I'd have been out of that room. Jean would have survived, and I would be exposed.*

I recognized the name on the phone Jean had uttered his last words into. It was his brother, a lesser known but well-off gentleman back in France. I'd have to do some careful research on him, but the name alone doesn't send off any alarms. But no matter what, when the investigation starts, the police will have a lead.

I'm going to have to grease some palms in the NYPD to take the heat off me.

As I slip out of the ridiculous outfit I had to don

for the evening, I stare out the windows in the living room, watching the city skyline in the distance.

Does being so cold really define my skill?

I was distracted by the thoughts of the bed I shared with Cassie earlier today, that much was without question. But putting that man down after he had been allowed to victimize a woman not at all unlike my new wife, knowing that I was saving Sonya's life by my actions...I felt a unique purpose in executing Jean Bouchard that was new to me entirely.

I've defined my career by my coldness. Just a killer from Siberia, I've been a lone attack dog for so long. But how long can I be so detached? How long before I'm called upon to take another life like the one I spared in the beach house?

The last of my clothes stripped from my body, I quietly get into bed alongside Cassie. Unconsciously, she presses herself into me as I take up space on the bed, her body warming my side as I get comfortable.

I pause for a moment, then slip my arm around her, and she murmurs quietly in her sleep.

*No. I can't be cold forever.*

I cannot continue as a mere killing machine when there are men alive in the world of the kind that would sell women like cattle. Who would push them to the limits of their lives for prestige.

*Who would buy a young woman like Cassie.*

My hand clenches around the sheets briefly as I

remind myself of my own complicity, and I glance at the outline of Cassie in the dark.

I can tell myself I'm better than some other dreg all I want, but I still bought this woman. So if I am to be her husband, I'm going to bring her every pleasure I can afford her. If her sweetness was what affected my work so dramatically, I will make it grow and thrive.

And if I'm truly sick of working for the lowest of the low in this city, maybe this fire will let me bring some justice to those who have it coming.

CASSIE

*A* sliver of fading moonlight through the lightly billowing curtains falls across my face, waking me up sometime before dawn. Once again, my half-asleep brain expects me to be in my twin bed back in upstate New York, waiting for my mother to knock on my door and get me up to make breakfast. But I don't hear anything but the constant hum of life from the city streets several stories down. Even in the near-total darkness, my eyes begin to adjust to the lack of light. I glance sidelong at the curtained window and see the faintest glow of moonlight mingled with neon lights and sleepless billboards, night-shift workers working by lamplight through wide, executive windows. Then my eyes turn to the space beside me in the massive bed,

There is a solid few inches of clear space between

my body and the one next to me, and I realize with a jolt that I have tangled myself up in the entire blanket, leaving my new husband's shirtless body completely uncovered. He's obviously made no attempt to steal the sheets from me, letting me sleep comfortably while goosebumps rise along his limbs from sleeping in the cool air without a blanket. And the space between us sends a little vibration of appreciation through me, as it occurs to me that he has been lying perfectly straight and still, nearly on the edge of the bed, just so that he wouldn't touch my sleeping body and wake me up.

*Or perhaps*, a cruel voice in the back of my head suggests, *he is just so repulsed by me that he doesn't want to brush up against me in the night.*

I shake myself internally of that thought. He has married me. He has chosen me. So he must really want me — right? Then the events of last night come rushing back to me in a series of rapid-fire images and sound bytes: his face between my legs, my own cries of astonished pleasure, his words to me, low and possessive.

*I want* you.

I swallow hard, my eyes lingering on the chiseled outline of Andrei's muscular stomach and chest. Last night I didn't get to see any of this, the hard abdominals and rock-hard chest, his bulging biceps and solid jawline. The soft, dim light plays along the contours of his handsome face. Even in sleep, his expression is cold and hard. I almost want to reach out and touch his full, sensual lips, run my finger along his straight nose and heavy brow. I want to smooth away the slight worry lines and convince his beautiful mouth to smile.

But instead, I slowly sit up in bed and look down at myself.

I have to suppress a gasp at the sight of my totally naked body.

I cannot believe I have slept next to a man in the same bed without any clothes on! My mother would be so disappointed, my father enraged! But then, I think bitterly, they are the ones who forced me into a smelly basement in only my underwear, surrounded by revolting men.

Except for one man. The one who saved me.

Or did he? Perhaps he was just another bidder, surveying me like a customer at the butcher, appraising each pound of flesh with a detached hunger...

Biting my lip, I feel a lump rising in my throat and tears stinging in my eyes again. It isn't fair. All the other girls in the congregation have been married off to men we all *knew*. Upright, conservative, godly men who wore khakis and sweaters and sang in the choir. Men who would surely avert their eyes and condemn the very sort of meat market I was pushed into. I've spent my entire life waiting for my Prince Charming, and now I'm stuck with this dark, ominous man I first saw in a dark and terrifying basement. This is not at all how I envisioned my life.

Getting out of bed carefully so as not to wake Andrei, I quietly pad out of the room, searching for a bathroom. When I walk into the living room, my stomach drops as my eyes land on the huge, floor-to-ceiling window across the room. A flash of last night invades my brain and I recall the cold glass against my spine, my new husband kneeling between my thighs, his tongue eliciting such sensations from my nether parts that I never thought possible.

I shudder to myself, thinking of how many transgressions against God I have made in this past week alone. Naked in front of men. Impure thoughts. Resentment toward my mother and father. Forgetting to pray. Marrying a man who doesn't seem to be of my faith…

One solitary, insistent tear finally escapes to roll down my cheek as I fumble for the bathroom door handle. Pushing inside, I pat at the wall in the darkness until I find the light switch and flip it up. My mouth falls open the second the light illuminates the room.

This is the biggest, most luxurious bathroom I have ever seen.

My eyes must be the size of saucers as I walk slowly around the room, my hands roving over every polished edge. This bathroom is bigger than my bedroom back home, with the bricked left and right walls lined by gray stone counters, deep marble sinks, and brushed metal finish, with mirrors perched over the length of the counters. The floor is made up of some kind of dark gray stone, cut irregularly to give it a natural, outdoorsy look. The light fixture above my head, in the center of the ceiling, is a heavy-looking, impressive candle chandelier. At the end of the room is an elaborate stone shower with multiple spigots and a massive, deep bathtub big enough to comfortably fit at least three people.

Not that three people should ever sit in a bath together.

With awe, I walk over to the bathtub and, after having to examine it for a couple minutes to figure out how it works, I turn both spigots to start the flow of water. I search under the counters and find a stack of neatly-folded, fresh-smelling black towels. This is the warmest room in the apartment so far, in both temperature and ambiance. I wonder if Andrei ever uses this bathtub, or if he is strictly a showering kind of man. It is difficult to picture him sinking into a bubble bath, that hard body and solemn face sinking in among the floral-scented bubbles.

A smile twitches at my lips, but fails to follow through.

To my dismay, I am unable to find any bubble bath, anyway. So I settle for a hot, bubble-less bath, taking a bar of very standard, utilitarian soap from the shower. It looks like the kind of soap one would use to remove excessive gunk, as for someone with a very dirty, grimy job. My mother used to buy soap similar to this for my little brother, as he was a particularly messy child, always jumping into mud puddles and playing with bugs. A twinge of heartbreak hits me then, imagining Isaiah with dirt smeared across his chubby cheek, a mischievous grin on his lips, revealing a gap where his two front baby teeth fell out.

I sink into the bath and splash my face with hot water, letting it mix with my tears. I miss him more than anything else. I wish so badly I could run to his room and hug him, read him his favorite passages, tickle him and make him burst into those infectious peals of laughter I love so much. Under our roof, there was always an air of sternness, of still and slightly oppressive calm. But Isaiah broke the silence — he was loud, he was rambunctious, and he injected some much-needed joy into our household.

I miss him dearly. I wonder to myself who will hug him and swing him around now? Who will make him grilled cheese sandwiches and read nursery rhymes in silly voices? I know my mother loves him, and she will keep him properly fed and clothed and cared for, enough to maintain his health

and appearance. But she is not particularly affection-
ate. Isaiah is a difficult child at times, and I worry
that she will not be able to tame him on her own, or
that my father will step in to beat him into shape.

The thought almost makes me want to jump out
of the bath and run all the way back to upstate New
York and scoop Isaiah up in my arms, keep him safe.

But I know that isn't an option. I am a married
woman now, at eighteen years old, and I cannot play
caretaker to my baby brother anymore. I have
someone else to care for and attend to — my
husband. I only wish I knew how to do that.

He is so strong and silent that I wonder if he even
*has* needs. Surely he feels lonely sometimes, living all
alone in this big, beautiful apartment, in this relentless and anonymous city. But he seems so put-
together. How can I possibly contribute to his life-
style in any meaningful way? He appears, for all
intents and purposes, to be doing perfectly well
without me. As far as I know, he doesn't have a maid
or a cook or anyone to keep his home for him. I am
shocked at the idea of a man taking care of his own
home without a woman's help.

And the apartment is flawless! All my life I have
been trained to cook, clean, and serve. But how can I
do any of those things where they aren't needed or
even requested?

But then, I remind myself darkly, there are other
needs a man must satiate.

Ones that I have not been educated about at all.

I can clean a house, cook a meal, and wait on a man hand and foot but I don't know the first thing about pleasing a man... *sexually*. And last night, I never even got the chance. Or did I? A feeling of shame and regret passes over me. It was our wedding night and I was the only one who had received any pleasure! And my pleasure is irrelevant! A woman is not meant to feel such ecstasy — it is her duty to serve, not to *be serviced*! Perhaps I only misread the signals, missed my cue. Maybe Andrei was hoping I would return the favor somehow, instead of lazily letting him do all the work.

My first night as a wife and I was already drenched in failure!

I cover my face with my hands and cry, letting the pent-up emotions finally bubble out of me, the tears streaking down my knuckles and into the bath water. I sit that way for quite some time, my shoulders shaking, my knees pulled to my chest, my long blonde hair floating like a massive halo around me in the water.

"What's the matter?" asks a deep, throaty voice from the doorway.

Startled, I let out a gasp and wrap my arms around my knees, trying unsuccessfully to cover my exposed body in the bath. Andrei is standing near the door, even taller and broader than I remember. His black hair is slightly ruffled from sleep and his eyes have the faintest of dark half-moons below them. There's stubble shadowing his jaw and his muscles ripple as he moves toward me slowly, with some trepidation.

"I — I hope I didn't wake you," I reply weakly, my voice thin and warbling from tears.

He stops suddenly and cocks his head ever so slightly, surveying me with an expression bordering almost on pity. I can see a flash of something like regret flicker in his eyes. Then he averts his gaze and keeps walking closer.

"You didn't," he answers simply, refusing to look at me even as he sits down on the edge of the bathtub. He passes a large hand back over his hair and lets out a heavy sigh. Then he asks, with genuine concern, "Why are you crying?"

"It's nothing," I assure him, hastily wiping my face. "I'm alright. Just washing off."

He starts to turn his eyes toward me again, then stops and shuts them. "May I — may I look at you?" he asks gruffly.

My heart swells a little at how gentlemanly he is. The rush of sudden affection I feel causes my lips to form the word, "Yes."

With that, Andrei turns to fix his eyes on mine, his nearly-black gaze locking on me. To my surprise, I don't feel ashamed to have him look at my naked body curled up like this. There is no cruelty, no disgust, no admonishment in his expression. He simply looks at me like I am fully-clothed, like I'm a regular person deserving of respect.

"I guess I'm a little homesick," I admit finally.

Andrei nods slowly.

"I understand that," he replies after a long pause.

I tilt my head to the side and, without thinking about it much, I reach for his hand. He doesn't seem to mind that my hand is wet and pruny as he takes it in his.

"Where is your home?" I press, truly interested. I wonder what kind of land must produce a man like Andrei, all rugged lines and dark countenance.

"Siberia," he answers.

I can feel my eyes growing large at this answer. I remember seeing the wide expanse of Siberia on world maps in my geography textbooks. It's always been a total mystery to me, and in fact, I didn't know that anyone really lived there. I've generally assumed it to be inhabited only by the occasional bear or reindeer.

"Really?" I ask breathlessly, staring up at him expectantly.

"I come from the coldest region inhabited by mankind," he says.

"How cold?" I sit up straighter and move closer.

Andrei looks at me thoughtfully for a moment before stroking the hair back out of my face and caressing my cheek. Instinctively, I first wince at his touch before leaning into it. I am not used to such tender, intimate gestures. But I think I will probably love getting used to it.

"In my homeland, it is so cold in the winter that the air will freeze solid in your lungs if you dare draw a breath outside," he explains, a twinkle of nostalgia in his eyes.

"How did you survive?"

He chuckles, a pleasant sound, surprising to hear from him. "Well, I held my breath and wore a lot of layers. Besides, it was all I ever knew back then."

"Do you miss it? Do you miss your parents?" I ask, leaning forward to rest my chin on his boxers-clad thigh. He stiffens a little and I worry that it's because of me.

But then he explains, "My mother and father died when I was very young."

I sit back and hang my head in apology. "I shouldn't have asked. I'm sorry."

Andrei takes my chin to tilt my head up and face him.

"You are my wife. You don't have to apologize for asking about my past."

At those words — 'my wife' — I feel my heartbeat quicken.

After a couple moments I add, "How do you deal with it? The homesickness, I mean."

He gives me a sympathetic look. "I can take you to a place I go to forget my pain."

"Where is it?" I ask.

Andrei gets up and hands me the black towel from the counter. "Dry off and get dressed and I will show you around the city. New York may not be the home I remember, nor is it the one you know, but it is the home we share together now. And it isn't as bad as it may seem. I promise you that."

ANDREI

"*I*'m not sure it's the best fit, Cassie…"

"Oh, it'll be fine, those big jackets of yours are supposed to cover everything to keep you warm, right?"

I try not to smile in bemusement as I watch Cassie struggle to pull one of my massive winter coats over her shoulders. It nearly engulfs her entire body, and as she pulls the hood up over her head, it falls over her eyes, and I can't hold back a laugh.

It's mid-morning, and I'm taking Cassie out.

"Perhaps we should do some clothes shopping while we're in the city," I venture. I figure it's about time for this poor girl to experience a little more style than what her father and mother picked out for her.

She's wearing one such ensemble under my jacket, and it's a bit like looking at a sepia-toned antique photo. A long brown skirt runs down to touch the knees, and a beige sweater covers up most of that. Her shoes are a little clunky, and her socks aren't nearly long enough to cover her shins. Even that bit of exposed skin manages to make her look modest.

"Brighton Beach is still NYC, so if you're going to live down here, you might like to dress the part," I add on.

"Well what's wrong with this?" she cries, pulling the hood down and sticking her lip out at me in protest. "I know it isn't the most modest thing in the world, but everyone at church seemed okay with it."

I raise my eyebrows at her and help her find her way out of my jacket. "Yes, well, I think you might like a little more variety than the one suitcase you brought with you. A husband ought to provide for his wife, don't you think?"

I see the hint of a smile play across her lips, and she bats her eyelashes up at me, though I don't think she realizes she's doing it. "Alright. One store."

THE LOWER EAST SIDE is already bustling with activity at this hour, and Cassie can't seem to tear her eyes away from the window.

I can't help but chuckle, glancing over at her awestruck expression.

"Don't laugh," she chides, though she quickly bites her lip in embarrassment, before adding on more reverentially, "I hardly left my own neighborhood is all."

"Well don't lose all your energy taking in the crowds, we aren't even at the Orchard Street district yet."

She tilts her head at me curiously, and as she opens her mouth, I cut her off before the question escapes her lips.

"No, it isn't an apple farm, it's just a shopping area."

A few minutes later, we've parked, and even as Cassie walks with both her arms wrapped around one of mine as she shivers in the brisk air, her eyes are wandering all over the scenery around her.

The Historic Orchard Street district is busy, but the commotion only adds to the powerful heartbeat of the area.

"Andrei, this place is like something out of a movie! I didn't even know you could put this many clothing stores in one place! Don't they all just end up selling the same kind of stuff?"

"You didn't go on shopping trips with your mother very much, did you?"

"No, most of it came from church yard sales, why?"

I laugh and hold her tighter to me, and she gives an adorable little squeak as I half-lift her up off the ground. I can only imagine what a magical experience the sights and sounds of this place must be for her.

The internationality of the area is what really seems to grab her. I let her gently tug at my arm lead us to just about every window on the stretch of street we walk down, and she indulges nearly every beckoning merchant urging us to come see their wares.

I find myself smiling a little more with each distraction. She begs me to take her into a little Turkish coffee shop, and a moment later, I'm trying to warn her not to burn herself on the bitter drink she's never tasted before. I end up drinking most of hers for her, but even the little bit she gets into her system puts an extra spring in her step.

She seems to have boundless energy, but small as she is, her teeth keep chattering, so I stop at one of the cart vendors and let her pick out a hand-knit scarf to wrap herself in. She chooses a pink and white one with little pom-poms on the tassels, and I show her how to wrap it properly so it fits snug, but not too tight.

After what feels like hours, I feel her slowing down at my side.

"What's the matter, coffee crash hitting you already?"

"Hm? Oh, oh no, nothing," she waves off, but I notice that she was looking towards one of the shops, and I follow her gaze. There's a large clothing boutique on a street corner, and there are elaborate designs adorning the legion of mannequins in the windows.

"You like the clothes there?" I ask, smiling.

"No, no," she backpedals quickly, "I mean, they look kind of nice, but I don't think they're the most appropriate things in the world, you know."

"But you like them," I press with a teasing grin, and she blushes a little.

"Well, I've never worn anything quite like that before, but I'm a married woman, and I really shouldn't be dressing like that in public, and —"

I bring us to a halt and hold her shoulders with both hands, looking down at her rather seriously, though not harshly. "Cassie, I may be your husband, but whether you're married or not, the only thing you should be wearing is exactly what you feel like wearing."

The poor girl wrings her hands for a moment, but the smile tugging at her face tells all, and after a moment of chewing on her lip as she plays with the idea, she nods vigorously.

"Okay, but just for a little bit!"

With that, she leads me by the hand into the boutique.

The place is a jungle of elaborate fabric. It's clearly some kind of up-and-coming designer trying to break out of its independent phase, and by the looks of the store, it's well on its way.

"A little bit" turns into nearly an hour of Cassie tearing through the store, brimming with renewed energy, eyes sparkling the whole time. I anticipate feeling bored at the display, but there's something peculiarly endearing about her enthusiasm as she brings up dresses and hats for me to look at — nearly half the store's worth.

"You seem to have an affinity for lace," I remark, and it's no exaggeration. Cassie has been gravitating towards frilly, lacy dresses, high stockings, and enormous bows.

"Well, these dresses feel like, I dunno," she twists her shoe into the ground as she tries to think of the expression, "makes me feel like a princess."

"Well, *printsessa*," I bow my head with teasing reverence, "would you like to try some of those royal dresses on?"

"It's after ten o'clock — isn't that a little late to go out?" I ask anxiously from my perch on a bench inside the massive walk-in closet. After a few hours in Central Park earlier, we came home to freshen ourselves up and put away all the masses of new clothes sent to the apartment from the many shops we frequented today. Until I saw them all in one place, I didn't realize just how much we bought. When we arrived back at the apartment building, there was a veritable mountain of packages waiting to be received in the lobby's holding area. The poor desk clerk had to call down two assistants to help us carry everything to the elevator and down the hall.

Andrei stands in the bathroom around the corner, checking his reflection, as though he could possibly look anything but handsome. He calls out, "Is this a late night for you?"

"Well, yes!" I answer, crinkling my nose. I can't believe people actually go out this late at night instead of just sleeping. My father used to always say that the dark hours are when temptations are most abundant, and that only 'loose women and whore-mongers' went out late at night.

I suppose tonight I am going to be a loose woman.

Standing up and biting my lip as I look down at the clothes I'm wearing, I know that my father would have some choice words to say about my appearance, as well. I've never before gone out with so much of my skin showing. I'm wearing all new items purchased today, and I feel violently self-conscious in them.

I also feel kind of pretty.

The dress I'm wearing is lavender-colored, flouncy, and falls to just above my knees. I've paired it with knee-high, frilly, white socks and pale pink shoes with slight heels to them. I shake my hair out of its messy bun so that it cascades in soft, full waves around my shoulders. Today, I saw so many beautiful women everywhere with their immaculate hair, chic ensembles, and flawless makeup, and now I feel self-conscious about the fact that I lack all of those things.

Certainly, back home I never felt attractive in any real way, but I also didn't feel ugly. The standards were simply different in the community I'm used to. Women are less adorned, but they are still expected to be soft and unsullied, totally put-together, even in their modest simplicity. Nobody really wore makeup or flashy clothing, but even our plain looks had to be perfectly arranged to suit the ideal: a clean, subservient, quietly pretty woman willing to obey without question or hesitation. Always willing to follow light-footed in the shadows of a man. We were the little brown birds meant to keep the nest and wait on the scarlet-hued males.

But here, in the big city, women wore the bright colors. The streets of New York are a veritable rainbow of different types of fashion and beauty. I never knew this many options even existed! I always learned that there is only one kind of acceptable look, and it's the same one every girl and woman back home adheres to. The same one I always wore, too.

And now, I look at myself in the floor-length mirror hanging on the back of the closet door and gasp at the sight. My body is adorned in such jewel-like colors, shiny and complex fabrics and textures, unlike anything I've ever seen, much less worn. The girl in the mirror looks like some stranger, even though my face is the same. Like my face has been cut and pasted onto some other girl's body. I am suddenly acutely aware of the fact that there is no makeup on my face. Prior to coming into New York

City, I never even considered it necessary or even desirable.

Makeup, my father says, is just an earthly tool meant to deceive and ensnare the weak-hearted. But what I saw today has opened my mind and given me a different perspective. I see the way people use clothing and makeup to express themselves, and I wonder if it can be yet another way to explore the glory of what God has created in the human race.

I'm interrupted from my reverie by Andrei's knock on the closet door.

"Are you ready?" asks his deep voice from the other side of the door, and I feel a wave of nervous nausea rush over me. I don't think I'll ever be ready. But I slowly open the door anyway, and when Andrei sees me, he almost cracks a smile.

Almost. But that hard expression hardly twitches at all, even though his eyes do soften a bit when they look me up and down. I find myself wanting more than anything to bring more softness into his life. I want him to be happy and light and warm, and I am determined to give him a million reasons to feel those things.

"I think so," I answer bashfully, looking down at my new shoes.

"You look lovely."

My eyes snap up at the compliment and I'm unable to suppress a wide grin, my cheeks getting flushed. He is my husband and I want to please him

SOLD TO THE HITMAN

for that reason, but there is also a genuine, organic desire growing in me to gain his approval, to be what he wants.

What he paid for.

"Thank you."

He has something in his hands, I realize, and I blink. "What's that?" It looks like a little black square that he's holding somewhat awkwardly, like he isn't used to it.

"A Kindle," he says in his light accent, and hearing it come from his voice makes me smile a little. "I'm sure you spent some moments reading with all that time to yourself, so I thought..." He trails off and ends up simply holding the little e-reader out to me. "It apparently can hold tens of thousands of books, and I already entered my payment details, so you can buy whatever you like."

"Th-thank you," I say as I take it into my hands and look it over, a little taken aback, but honestly, part of me wants to jump in bed with it immediately. We'd had nothing like that back home, but I was always fascinated by the idea of a tiny little device that could hold such a wealth of information.

He offers his arm to me a little stiffly, looking like a rugged, bad-boy prince in his black leather jacket, pressed white button-up shirt, and dark jeans. I hesitantly take his arm, then lean into him a little more, trying to relax. After all, we did spend the whole day together.

And last night we were awfully close…

"So where exactly are we going?" I ask him as I set the Kindle aside for later while he silently drapes a new brown peacoat over my shoulders. He leads me out into the hallway and into the elevator, dodging the question until the elevator doors close.

Then he says quietly, "We're going to a place where I feel a little more at home."

"But where is that?"

Andrei gives me a sidelong glance, his dark eyes falling on me and sending a little thrill down my spine. There is just something so mysterious and enigmatic about his eyes — that spellbinding, soul-reading, black stare.

Again, surrounded by the mirrored walls of the elevator chamber, I am startled by how sharply our looks contrast. Every aspect of his countenance is dark, heavy, nearly predatory. Beside him, I am pastel and dreamy-eyed, a pale waif sharing the air with a big, bad wolf.

"Aren't you going to tell me? Is it a secret?" I press him, cocking my head to the side.

Finally, when we get into his Corvette and he starts the engine, he answers me.

"We're going to a place called Brighton Beach. There's a large population of *Russkiys* living in the area."

A beach? I am definitely confused now. I know that I have led a very sheltered life, and there is so much I don't know about the world, but it seems very unusual to go out to a beach in the middle of the night when it's this cold out.

"Brighton Beach?" I repeat, furrowing my brow. "Isn't it... isn't it a little cold?"

"What do you mean?" Andrei says, glancing over at me with a bemused expression.

I fidget with the hem of my dress, biting my lip. I can't tell if he is joking or not. Everyone back upstate is very straightforward. We don't joke around. So I'm not particularly skilled at determining when people are being facetious, but I feel that he *must* be, right now.

"It's dark out, and cold, and I — I don't know how to swim!" I ramble all at once, closing my eyes and folding my hands in my lap.

Andrei snorts and I open my eyes to see him giving me a bemused look.

"What's so funny?" I ask, starting to feel a little miffed.

"We're not going to *the* beach — we're going to a bar."

"Called Brighton Beach?"

Andrei swipes a hand over his face, clearly amused. "No, the bar is called the Amber Room, and it is located in Brighton Beach."

Suddenly, I feel like the dumbest, most ignorant human being currently breathing air. I'm thankful for the darkness, because I can feel my cheeks burning bright pink.

"Oh," I say softly.

For the rest of the drive, we sit mostly quiet except for my occasional comments about the scenery and signs we pass by. Andrei is cordial and kind, but not very responsive, and certainly never forthcoming. He is rather like my father in this one, singular way. Both are quite reticent — men of little words. But when they do speak, they are charismatic. People stop to listen.

I, on the other hand, am a complete chatterbox. I hope that I'm not bothering Andrei with my unending commentary, but I have a tendency to talk too much when I get nervous. And every moment I spend in this revealing dress, in an unfamiliar city, with a handsome but intimidating man, at this late hour... my nerves are totally on edge.

By the time we reach our destination, I feel quite sick to my stomach. There are people walking around outside, lining up to get in the door. The building itself is fairly nondescript, but Andrei insists that this place makes him feel at home, so I want to give it a fair chance. I am eager to find out more about my new husband: what he likes, what he thinks about, what his memories are filled with. Despite our legal union, we are hardly more than strangers, but I am determined to break down his walls.

Most of the people here tower over me, the women teetering on high heels, the men tall and well-dressed, a lot of them with tattooed arms. I have to fight to keep my expression neutral, to suppress the urge to let my mouth fall open and gawk. *This* is Andrei's kind of crowd?

My husband is guiding me to the front of the line, garnering us some bitter scowls from those waiting to get in. I whisper to Andrei, "Don't we need to go to the back of the line?"

"The owner's husband is an old business contact of mine," he replies simply.

I feel like that may not be a sufficient excuse, but I don't say a word. The burly guy at the door gives Andrei a nod and lets us through without hesitation, causing some guys to angrily shout, "Hey!" from behind us.

"Oh, settle down," orders the door guy, without even looking up from his phone.

Once inside, we walk down a curving corridor. I am immediately assaulted by the sensation of pounding, pulsating music. The deep, reverberating bass and the fast pace of the music makes me feel instantly out of place. I've never listened to anything but classical music and hymns, as my father always insists that "popular music is the root of sin in today's youth culture" and therefore, all access to radio and television media were very restricted. I've also never seen this many people in one place, this close together, moving like this.

Dancing.

I cling helplessly, fearfully to Andrei's side. I have never been allowed to dance or to watch anyone else dance. It is a direct path to temptation and sin. It's utterly immoral for people to move together this way! At least, that's what I've been told my whole life.

Perhaps Andrei picks up on my intense fear, because he wraps an arm around me in a surprising gesture of protection and warmth, his fingers gently brushing through my hair.

"Is it too much?" he asks, leaning in close so I can hear his voice through the deafening music. I shrug and shake my head, not wanting to admit my true feelings. He raises an eyebrow at my silence, clearly not convinced, and guides me through the crowd to a counter where lots of people are seated on glossy bar stools. There are shelves upon shelves of multi-colored bottles of varying shapes and sizes.

Alcohol. Another vestige of a sinful world. 'The devil's drink,' my father calls it.

I gulp back my fear as Andrei muscles us through the throngs of swaying, laughing people to get us about a foot's width of space at the counter. His arm is crooked around me, accidentally pinning me against the bar. A tall, pretty girl with cropped hair dyed blue at the tips is working the counter, taking incomprehensible drink orders from the already-buzzed crowd with a cool, collected ease.

When she catches sight of Andrei, she does a double-take, then gives him a familiar nod and smirk. She slides over and says, "Long time no see! Been busy lately?"

Before he can answer, her eyes fall on me and her smile widens. "Guess that answers my question. What's your name, sweetheart?"

I struggle to make my voice heard over the pounding din. "C-Cassie."

"Nice to meet ya, I'm Natalie. Whatcha drinkin' tonight, hon?"

Andrei interjects, "She's underage, Natalie. But she'll have a cranberry juice, and I'll have a — "

"Yeah, yeah, vodka tonic. Creature of habit, this one," the bartender adds to me.

She turns and prepares our drinks so quickly it astounds me, then spins back to us and sets it on the bar counter with a smile. When Andrei tries to hand her cash, she purses her lips and shakes her head.

"Nah, you know it's on the house. Have a good time! And look after Miss Cassie here," Natalie tells him with a wink. Andrei lifts his drink in a kind of casual salute and guides me back away to a corner table, the two of us skirting the dance floor.

"You must be very popular," I remark.

Andrei shrugs. "Like I said, this place is the most like home for me."

"Is Natalie from Siberia, too?" I ask genuinely.

He chuckles and takes a sip of his drink. "No, no. But I am a regular here."

"What does that taste like?" I gesture shyly toward his vodka tonic.

Offering the little glass to me, he says, "Try it for yourself."

"But… I'm underage," I protest, even as I take the glass from him.

"It's only a taste," Andrei counters.

My father's voice in the back of my head shouts at me sternly, urging me to put the glass down and resist temptation. Instead, I raise it to my lips and take the tiniest of sips. I immediately grimace at the bitter taste. A shudder runs through my body and Andrei looks like he might actually crack a smile.

"Don't like it?"

Not wanting to seem rude, I deny it. "N-no, it's… it's good." To prove my point I take a big, long gulp of the disgusting clear liquid and have to fight to keep it down.

Andrei reaches over and takes the drink back, his full lips finally breaking into a rare, captivating smile. "How do you feel?"

The effect is instantaneous. My head gets fuzzy and my limbs tingle. I almost want to laugh, for no real reason except that I feel pretty darn good. I lick my lips and can't help but notice the way Andrei's eyes dart to my mouth when I do it. That makes me feel some kind of warm sensation between my legs, and suddenly I want to do something crazy.

I want to dance.

Hopping down from the high-top bar stool, I reach for Andrei's hand, swaying ever so slightly on my feet. He gives me a questioning look, but when I tug on his sleeve, he tosses back the rest of his drink in one deep draught, gets to his feet, and allows me to lead him into the pulsating throng of dancers.

My heart hammers in my chest. That warning voice in my mind is hissing at me to resist, resist, resist! But the alcohol combined with the hard, warm body of the man behind me radiates a numb determination around my body and I just need to *move*. We weave through the crowds to where the music beats loud and rhythmic above us and all around us, the bassline thumping alongside my heart. The conscious part of my brain is floundering because I don't know *how* to dance. But some subconscious instinct takes over and seizes my limbs, making me sway, then raise my arms above my head and roll my hips side to side.

As though pulled by invisible marionette strings, I start to move with the music, and Andrei slides in close behind me, his arms coming down to keep me near. His large hands fall to my waist, rocking me, gently controlling the rhythm of my movements. I can feel his ticklish, vodka-tinged breath on my cheek, his lips brushing along the slope of my neck to press soft, teasing kisses against my jaw. His hands slide up and down my frame, squeezing my thighs, roving up my stomach to subtly brush over my breasts. The music, the sensation of his body against mine, and the intoxicating drink are sending me into a confusing state.

I'm dizzy and frightened and exhilarated all at once. I can feel a wetness growing between my thighs and suddenly I can't stop myself from spinning around to face Andrei. I tilt my head up to look at him, peering into his dark eyes, his solid features, and my hands both go up to bring his face down closer to mine...

So I can kiss him.

At first, my lips are closed tight, and a cold nervousness threatens to unravel the moment. But then I remember that this is my *husband*. He chose me. And he wants me. My lips part and my tongue prods into his mouth, and he answers with the same. His hands slide into my hair and along my lower back, pulling me into him so that I can feel every rippling, tensing muscle of his body against my own.

There's something long and hard against my leg, and I lean into it hungrily, without a single thought as to what it might mean. I kiss him in a way I never knew was possible for me. I kiss him like I've never seen before, save for one time...

My mind flashes momentarily back to the most scandalous thing I've ever seen, a memory which has sustained my flickering desires for love for years. I was fourteen, and it was one of the rare times when my mother allowed me to visit the park with her and Isaiah, who was only a toddler then. He threw his ball, which rolled down a hill, and I went to fetch it for him.

At the bottom of the hill, several yards from where the ball had stopped rolling, there was a willow tree by a pond. Beneath the graceful, slim branches of the willow lay a couple, tangled up in each other's arms and legs, their lips locked together in a passionate kiss. They were fully clothed, but there was such an obvious heat between them that they might as well have been naked, the only two human beings left in the world. They did not acknowledge me, and even though I knew it was a sin, I stood entranced, watching them for several minutes until my mother came looking for me. When she saw what I was looking at, she yanked me away by the arm, scolding me for being a voyeur, urging me to beg God's forgiveness.

After that, I was never allowed to go to the park with them again, instead having to stay home and practice my piano lessons. But every time they went out and I was left alone at the black and white keys, my mind inevitably wandered back to that afternoon in the park. I wondered if I would ever know a passion like that.

And now, wrapped in Andrei's arms, I feel a

unique stirring deep inside me. It's happening — despite the grim circumstances of our union, despite his coldness and my fear, things are beginning to change. He's an imposing marble statue and I am a trembling, lost little girl, but he is beginning to thaw and I am finding my strength.

It's only the start. We hardly know each other. But I know this is real, whatever it is.

And when Andrei starts to guide me backward through the crowd and into a sequestered chamber near the back of the club, I don't resist. The sign on the door says VIP LOUNGE and when he opens the door, there's no one inside. As though fate itself has aligned to let us in, alone together at last.

He sits down on a plush red sofa and pulls me down to sit sideways on his lap, his mouth still devouring mine needily. When his hands slide up my thighs, I inhale sharply, and fear begins to sneak its ugly tendrils back through my mind. Surely he isn't going to touch me like he did before... not in a public place! This isn't what I ever envisioned for my first time. I suddenly feel so exposed, so uncertain, my former oblivious fog clearing away.

When his fingers brush over my panties underneath my dress, I break away with a jolt.

Andrei looks at me, his features hard and cold yet again.

I start to open my mouth to say something, but I don't know what to say. Suddenly, I am very afraid.

I've rebelled. I've teased him. I made him want me so badly and now I'm pushing him away! To serve and please my husband is my primary purpose in life, and now I'm screwing it all up. I remember my mother warning me, 'Do as your husband tells you, Cassandra. Even if you don't want to, you must always obey him, or he will be angry with you. The only way to protect yourself, to be a godly woman, is to do as he says.'

My heart pounds in my chest, waiting for his reaction.

A flicker of darkness crosses his face and I prepare for my punishment.

## ANDREI

*E*ach thump of her heart that I feel makes me want her more, and I sense her desire for me creeping out of the tight-knit cocoon she's spent so long bound up in.

I've never desired her so strongly. As my hands venture dangerously up her thighs, pushing away all the expensive lace that makes her all the more rare and precious, I hear soft moans escape her lips. And they seem to beg me to press onward.

I will make her first time worth remembering.

I'm looming over her like a ravenous predator, and as my hands explore her body, Cassie seems to be readying herself to be devoured, urging me forward. With a low growl in my chest, I wrap my hands around her hips and move in to give her all that she could possibly want...

But she recoils.

The way she moves is unmistakable—I feel her limbs pull into her body, moving away from me instinctively, and as I freeze in place, still as a statue, I look into those large, shining eyes of hers and see the telltale glint of fear in their pupils. She fears me.

A true lamb cowering before a wolf.

"Cassie," I say in a whisper, drawing back ever so slightly, "*printsessa*, what's the matter? Do you not want this?"

Her voice cracks as she struggles for words tragically.

"I..." Before she can continue, her cheeks flush an even deeper red, and she turns her face away from me, shame mixing with her terror as she curls up tight into herself on the couch.

My heart sinks, and I realize that I've pushed her too far. Maybe this young woman truly isn't ready for such an experience, not so soon after escaping the stiflingly repressive world she was reared in.

"Cassie, I know I may seem frightening to you still," I say gently as her eyes flit back to me briefly, "but I only wish to bring you pleasure—and there's so much of it just within reach. But I would never force you to do something you don't fully desire."

"No!" she gasps, looking suddenly panicked. "No no, I-I want this, I really do! Oh my gosh, I'm so sorry," she wrings her hands together. "I should never have said anything, I—I don't mean to make you think I…" She bites her lip, stumbling over her words.

"I just don't know if I'm ready," she finally lets out.

"Cassie…" I say to her in a low tone, and she looks up at me fearfully. I meet her gaze, even and unreadable, and I let the moment linger between us for an instant before continuing.

"You will never have to do anything you don't want to do. I didn't buy you for you to be my slave. All you have to say is stop, and I will. Cassie, you are more than just an object to me. You're a person, and you deserve to have a say in what happens in your life. I know you may have been taught only to obey, but from now on I want you to choose your own path. I will do everything in my power to make you happy, even if it means I never get to touch you again."

There were tears in her eyes already, but they well up to the point of bursting in the moment that follows, and before I know it, she throws her arms around me, embracing me tightly, and I slowly return the gesture, pressing my cheek against the top of her head.

Then I feel a kiss at my neck.

Her face has moved up from my chest, and her soft lips are pressed into my exposed skin, and as she lingers there for some time, I feel her hands exploring my torso with more bravery than before.

ALEXIS ABBOTT

I feel her heart on my chest again, thumping away, worked up into a storm as it tears itself apart between its repressed, chained-up desires and its need to free itself.

I move my face down to meet her, and with a newfound hunger I didn't know her to possess, she reaches up and wraps her hands around my head, hoisting herself up into a kiss.

It's deep and long, and she moves her lips against mine as though desiring so much more. I do not deny her. Sliding my hands around her waist, I let her meld into me, moving my tongue to her lips gently at first. As they part to let me in, I delve forward with abandon, and she meets me with just as much energy.

Now her gasps become desperate between kisses, and we become totally lost in one another as I feel her grasping at my clothes, climbing me needfully and hungrily.

"Andrei," she whispers into my ear as she rests her chin on my shoulder, letting my hands grasp her ass. "All my life, I've never felt like I've had a real choice in things. Even if I wanted something, I felt like it was decided before I was ever involved. With you, though..."

She moves back just enough to look me in the eyes, and I look upon her radiant features and feel my heart begin to melt.

"...I feel like I can finally *desire* and *choose* with you, Andrei."

"You deserve nothing but what you wish, *printsessa*," I whisper back in a husky voice.

"I admit," she says, "I'm...I'm still afraid, but I know for certain that I want this. I want this more than I've wanted anything in a long, long time."

My gaze boring into her, I ask, "Do you want *me*?" I take her hands and draw them across my body, feeling my rock-hard muscles, swollen with blood flow that she stirred up in me. Slowly, I trace her hands down towards my thighs, getting dangerously close to the stiff shaft between them. "Do you want everything you feel, everything my body can give you? Do you want all of that to be inside you, taking every ounce of you?"

"Yes," she breathes, "but I just don't know how. I've never even seen..." her voice trails off as her eyes fall on the bulge of my cock, the hard outline desperate to escape my pants.

I move in and kiss her again, my tongue swirling through her mouth, dancing with hers as we revel in one another's warmth.

"Don't worry," I assure her as we break. "I will teach you."

There's a long pause between us, and her eyelashes flutter after she steals another glance at my manhood.

"Will you show me tonight?"

CASSIE

The ride home from Brighton Beach is a whirlwind. Even though the drive there seemed to last forever, the trip back seems to pass by in the blink of an eye. Perhaps this is partly due to the fact that Andrei doesn't seem to pay any attention to traffic laws and speed limits on the way to the apartment building. The Corvette weaves nimbly in and out of traffic, down side streets and shortcuts, some probably at least borderline illegal, in order to get us home before our heads clear completely.

I wonder if Andrei feels the same way I do right now: all flaming nerves and skipping heart — but then I remember that he has probably done this before. It's a rather strange thought, that my husband has most likely touched other women before me. He is older than me, older than any of the young men from the congregation or the homeschooling community I previously viewed as contenders for my hand. And although I have not asked him outright, all signs point to the fact that he is not of my faith. Living outside the church, it can only be assumed that he has not been saving himself for marriage as I have.

As handsome as he is, I doubt he's had any difficulty finding women.

The thought of his hands on another woman's body, his lips on another woman's mouth, makes me want to cry. How can I possibly live up to what he has had before me? I don't know what I'm doing at all. Andrei plans to teach me, but what if I don't do it right?

These fears rocket through my head, plaguing my thoughts so fully that I block out the ride home. When the Corvette finally stops outside the building, my stomach churns. I want this — I want *him* — more than anything, but I'm just so scared.

Andrei turns to me, leans over the console, and takes my face in one big, strong hand. He gazes into my eyes for a long moment while I hold my breath in anticipation. Then he dives in to kiss me hard, his tongue pushing into my mouth and his fingers tracing down my cheek, my jaw line, my neck. I feel wanted. It's a foreign feeling, but I am beginning to crave it intensely.

Wordlessly, he gets out of the car and helps me out, as well, before taking me by the hand and leading me into the building. With a silent urgency we rush to the elevator. As soon as the doors close, he pins me between his body and the wall, kissing me and feeling me up. His manhood presses hot and hard against my hip and I rock into it, eliciting a groan from deep inside his throat.

The elevator doors open with a *ding* and he scoops me up so that my legs are wrapped around his waist, then carries me down the hall and into our apartment. He rips off my jacket and lets it fall to the floor, his lips never breaking away from mine. Without even flicking on the lights, he swings me around to perch me on the kitchen counter, his hands tugging at my dress to pull it up and over my head. I shiver in the cool air and lean into him self-consciously, not wanting him to look at my nearly-naked physique. I know he's seen it before, but I still feel so exposed and ashamed to be naked in the presence of a man, even if he is my husband.

But he refuses to indulge my modesty, pushing back to look me up and down, his eyes roving over every inch of me. I am wearing a pair of frilly, pink satin panties and an ivory-colored bra which Andrei selected for me in one of the boutiques we visited earlier. The cups of the bra are sheer, lined with lace and decorated with tiny rosettes, allowing for my rosy pink nipples to show through the fabric.

"*Krasivaya*," he murmurs, shaking his head and swiping a hand over his mouth.

"Wh-what does that mean?" I ask, starting to cover myself with my hands.

Andrei catches my wrists and pins them behind my back, leaning in to whisper in my ear, "It means you are beautiful."

"Am I?" My voice is breathless and soft.

"It is my intention to make you feel as lovely as you look," he promises, scooping me up again to carry me into the bedroom. He gently sets me down on the bed, smoothing down my hair and kissing me on the forehead.

Standing in front of me, my eyes are drawn to the bulge in the front of his jeans. It looks too enormous, too powerful, straining to break free from its constraints. I wonder what it feels like, what it will feel like inside me.

The very thought makes me wet.

Andrei catches me looking at him and says softly, "This really is your first time, isn't it?"

I nod, looking down at the floor a little ashamedly.

"Are you sure you're ready?"

"I — I think so. Yes."

He untucks his shirts and unzips his jeans slowly, sliding them down his thighs and stepping out of them. Then he shrugs off his jacket, and unbuttons his shirt it to toss it over his shoulder onto the floor. Standing nearly naked in just his silky black boxers, I gasp a little. Seeing him this way for the very first time is startling: all that muscle hinted at beneath his clothes is now exposed in front of me and I can scarcely believe he's real.

"You… you're so handsome," I breathe, my eyes wide. Hesitantly, I reach out and touch his taut stomach, every abdominal muscle sharply defined and rock-hard. There is a faint trail of dark hair leading down from his navel and disappearing into his boxers. I trace this downy path with one curious forefinger, stopping short at the waistband of his underwear.

But before I can withdraw my hand, Andrei takes hold of it and slides my hand down farther to brush over the massive bulge there. I gasp again, and cover my mouth with my other hand, even as my own private parts respond with a gush of wet warmth. I must be so slick down there by now, and Andrei has hardly even touched me at all.

Holding my breath, I trace the outline of his shaft through the fabric of his boxers, then I get a little braver and run my palm up and down its substantial length. Andrei groans his approval and pushes into me ever so slightly.

"Don't be afraid," he says kindly.

With that, I pull down his boxers and he steps out of them to stand totally naked before me, his colossal manhood jutting out, hard and engorged.

"Oh my — oh my gosh!" I exclaim. "It's so *big*."

"Touch it," Andrei says imperiously.

I am reluctant at first, intimidated by his size. But then curiosity and desire overcome me and I gently wrap my hand around his member, my fingers barely able to contain him. When he doesn't pull back, I decide to run my thumb around the head of his shaft slowly. Andrei closes his eyes and groans.

"*Da, malyshka.* Good girl."

His growl of approval sends me into a frenzy. Suddenly, I need him. Now.

"Please… I'm ready," I whisper. Andrei opens his eyes and immediately reaches behind me to unclasp my bra, then gently pushes me back to lie down on the bed. He tugs my panties down my legs and drops them on the floor before climbing over to straddle me. He positions himself between my legs, holding his member so that the head of his shaft rubs up and down my slick opening. My breath comes raggedly as I try to rock my hips up into him, needing more.

Andrei circles the little bundle of nerves at the top of my private parts and I shudder involuntarily, feeling close to a climax before he's even entered me. I am suddenly aware of the soreness between my legs — I am literally aching for him.

He leans over to kiss me again, softly at first, then with a relentless need.

"Please, oh please…" I moan between kisses.

And then it happens. The head of his member pushes into me and I cry out in surprise. My eyes roll back in my head as he rocks back and then pushes into me again and again, only pushing a centimeter or so farther each time. I glance down to see that he isn't even halfway sheathed inside me yet! I already feel so full, my virgin muscles stretching desperately to accommodate his massive size.

"Are you alright?" he asks, his voice raspy with need. I can tell that he is straining, using every ounce of his willpower to hold back, to keep from hurting me. From the lust burning in his dark eyes I can tell that it takes everything he has not to simply ram into me and split me in two.

I feel a rush of mingled desire and affection for this powerful, mysterious, shockingly considerate man I now call my husband.

"Yeah," I reply, the word scarcely more than a pronounced exhale.

And with that, he finally pushes into me completely, filling me to the hilt. A sharp wave of pain electrifies my body and I yelp in surprise and agony. Andrei's hands rush to stroke my face, his lips peppering my mouth and cheeks with kisses.

"Shh, I will go slowly," he assures me, resting his forehead against mine. He reaches down to gently circle the inflamed bundle of nerves between my legs, stroking me into a pleasurable oblivion even as his shaft breaks through the barrier and causes me to cry out in pain.

"*Ty v poryadke,*" he says soothingly, and I don't understand, but the foreign words soothe me.

He starts moving his hips, pumping into me very slowly and carefully at first. His thumb circling my tingling bud quickens its pace, and before long I can feel an orgasm approaching.

"Ohhh," I moan, tilting my head back as my body lurches upward of its own volition and my second climax shudders through my veins, despite the dulling pain.

"That's it, baby," Andrei mumbles, starting to move faster. "*Otlichno.*"

He grasps at the headboard, his control beginning to slip. His massive shaft pummels into me, hitting deep inside, filling me up until pain and pleasure reach identical heights. My fingers claw at his back needily, animalistic moans falling from my lips. Finally, I come again, warm honey gushing from between my legs as Andrei pushes into me again and again, my opening convulses around him.

With a few quick, frenzied snaps of his hips, Andrei thrusts hard into me one final time and bellows in ecstatic relief as he fills me up with a hot, thick stream of his seed.

"Ohh, *dorogaya...*" he moans, collapsing forward onto me, his forearms just barely bracing himself so he doesn't crush me with his massive chest. His eyes are tightly shut and his breath comes slowly and raggedly, the two of us panting in the charged silence between us. Then he opens his eyes, those dark orbs blazing with a quiet intensity. I stare at his face in wonder and awe — I feel as though suddenly everything has changed.

Am I a woman now?

What does this mean for the two of us?

Our marriage has been consummated! We are now bound to each other by a deeper, more binding connection than a simple piece of paper and an exchange of verbal vows. We are now interlocked, forever, soul *and* body. I belong to him, and not just because he bought me,

And he belongs to me.

Andrei surprises me with the tenderness of his next move. He leans forward to gently rest his forehead against mine, inhaling deeply as though trying to breathe me in. Holding himself up with one impossibly strong arm, his other hand comes up to lightly cup my cheek, his thumb passing fondly over my lips. Then he kisses me sweetly, his mouth just barely grazing mine in the most delicate of angel kisses.

"Are you alright, *lyubov moya*?" he asks, his voice so soft and full of genuine concern.

I nod, happy tears pooling in my eyes.

When he sees the shining moisture in my gaze, his face contorts into an expression of worry and he kisses my cheek. "*O net*, then why do you cry?"

A single tear escapes to roll down my cheek and neck as I lay perfectly still on the bed.

"I am so happy," I reply, my voice choked with

emotion. I feel so complete, so whole, so incredibly swathed in warm, unfailing love — for the first time in my life. I have never felt so close to another human being in all my years, and to think... I have only barely met him.

\* \* \*

WE SPEND the next morning in bed, being lazy and simply enjoying each other's presence. After our first time together, I am sore, my muscles aching and my newly-christened private parts unaccustomed to such exertion. When we finally get up, I am appalled to see a large bloodstain on the satin sheets from underneath me. I'm so shocked by the sight that I nearly faint, apologizing profusely for ruining the beautiful bedsheets. But Andrei assures me it's nothing to fret over, that we can just buy new ones. So he pulls the stained sheets off the bed, tosses them in the wash, and runs me a luxurious bath complete with candles and bubble bath he stashed away some time ago.

As I sit in the bath, sinking down into thick white foam that smells of roses and lavender, I smile to myself. I can't believe my luck. I know it can't be possible that every girl ends up with a man so strong and doting. I stay in the bath for a long time, my head leaned back and my muscles starting to loosen back up. The toasty water and floral scents soothe my aches and pains until I start to feel like my old self again.

Well, except for the fact that I can never *be* my old self again. I am a changed woman.

After my bath, I curl up on the couch with a blanket and watch television while Andrei orders us something called "take-out" for an early lunch. I don't even know what we're watching — it's a "soap opera" as Andrei calls it, with a cast of very dramatic, beautiful, immaculately-dressed characters who all seem to be either sleeping with or related to each other in one way or another. It's an eye-opening experience, watching TV for the first time without parental supervision. And this is a *real* show, not a news segment or a religious story.

"Do you like Chinese food?" asks Andrei, dialing a number into his cell phone.

I bite my lip, feeling very ignorant for the millionth time in the past few days. Yet another question I don't know the answer to. I shrug.

"I... I don't know. I've never had it before."

Andrei raises an eyebrow in a look I've been getting a lot from him lately. "You've never had Chinese food." He says it like a statement, rather than a question.

I shake my head sadly, fiddling with the blanket in my lap.

"Do you like chicken?"

"Yes."

"Rice?"

"Yes."

"Vegetables?"

"Of course."

"We can work with that."

When the food arrives, I have no idea what it is or where to begin. He hands me a pair of long, skinny wooden sticks and tells me to use them instead of a fork. I look at him like he's lost his mind, suspicious that he must be playing a trick on me. After he places his hand over mine and shows me how to place the chopsticks between my fingers and pinch pieces of chicken off the plate, I start to get the hang of it, though I never quite do it gracefully.

The rest of the day goes by smoothly, the two of us lounging around. In the afternoon, I fall asleep on the couch, and Andrei goes out to buy new bedsheets. When I wake up, he's come back and changed into an exceedingly handsome suit, his hair slicked back. He gently urges me to get up and put on a gorgeous gown we bought yesterday.

"Where are we going?" I ask, rubbing my eyes sleepily.

"Wake up, *sonnyy*, we're going to the opera."

My eyes go fully wide at this announcement and I immediately leap off the couch, rushing to get dressed. I have never been to an opera, and I have no idea what to expect. Once or twice, my mother left the radio unattended, and I heard a couple songs being belted out by women with powerful voices. I could never tell what they were saying, but that didn't subtract from the beauty in the least.

Andrei drives us to the massive, elaborate theater, my face frozen in an expression of over-whelmed awe the entire time. Andrei is gallant and prince-like in his suit, tall and noble in his bearing. I know everyone's eyes are on us, even in the context of the expensively-dressed, high-society crowd. We settle into our seats and watch the opera, his hand wrapped around mine.

It's an utterly magical night. I am amazed at the power and strength of the opera singers, the beauty of the sets, even the decorum of the audience. Every-thing is perfect, except…

During the third act, Andrei quietly disappears from my side, offering no excuse. He remains gone for quite some time. I am mostly too wrapped up in the gorgeousness of the opera to pay too much attention, but my husband's absence does ring like a strange alarm bell somewhere in the back of my mind. Something is off, but I don't know what, and I am too afraid to ask.

ANDREI

*I* hate to leave my wife alone, even in the safety of the opera house. But I have ulterior motives for coming here. My hit on the Frenchman was sloppy, the only kill I've botched since becoming a professional. So it tears at my mind.

There's no way I can risk exposing myself, not when Cassie's well-being is on the line, so I've had to look into matters carefully. Which means slowly. If word gets around that one of the *Bratva's* killers is looking into the hit, it'll incriminate me. And that's all it takes in my world to be undone. For good.

Finally a source turned up something, a Frenchman was in town with some pull, a rare thing. And he was at the opera, meeting with a powerful local connection about the death of his brother.

I make a detour along the private box seats until I

find exactly the one I am looking for. There, I can see the slickly dressed Frenchman, with his silver-frosted tips sat with a sour expression, talking to someone out of my view.

"Mon frère! My own brother, killed in your city," he says, anger welling up in the well-dressed European, his French accent thick as he spoke in English. "Killed by one of your own, a Russian," he says with such distaste.

"Not every Russian in the city is on our payroll," says the other voice, but I can't see the face of the man saying it, he's blocked by a red velvet curtain.

The Frenchman curses in his native tongue.

"That is not good enough, Kasym!" he says, but I don't recognize the name. "Not after all the shit I covered up for you in Paris, and beyond," he adds with such distaste. "You owe me. And more than that," he says, grinding his teeth.

"Don't say anything you'll regret, Pierre. I know," Kasym says, holding out a hand bedecked in more rings than any man ought to wear. "I will protect the flow of the goods. And if that means I have to gun down half my fellow *russkiye* to find the man who did your brother in, then I will. That is a promise."

Pierre stiffens a little, but then seems to soften, giving a nod to Kasym.

"I have looked over you a long time, on behalf of your father, I consider myself like an uncle. Do not let me down, Kasym. I want this man to suffer. To see everything he ever had taken from him. Anyone he has ever loved to die before his eyes, just as I heard my brother die."

"Now that, I would relish," Kasym says with a wicked laugh.

CASSIE

When Andrei returns, it is as though nothing has happened — except that his eyes have this faraway look, his face hardened against the world once more.

He still takes my arm with a soft touch, guiding me gently through the opera house as we navigate the post-show crowds back to the car. I close my eyes and pretend to be asleep on the ride home, though I occasionally sneak a one-eyed glance over at my husband in the passing neon lights intermingled with nighttime darkness.

There is something unnamed consuming him, preoccupying his mind. The thought that he is hiding something from me eats away at my newfound happiness, no matter how desperately I long to ignore it, to put it far from my mind so it can't plague my joyful heart.

I don't know what it is, and I dare not ask, afraid to shatter the illusion.

# ANDREI

*I* know I'm going to be easily the most down-dressed person at this party, but I don't like looking like a villain from some crime drama on television.

My car pulls up the long driveway after passing security, and for once, every other car on the lot is on par with mine — a lot of sports cars, a lot of black luxury sedans, and a handful of limousines.

I'm on the job again.

This contract could not have come at a more opportune time. Ever since my display at the auction where I bought Cassie, things have been somewhat tense with Sergei Slokavich, to say the least. He regards me with the air of caution he'd long ago thrown to the wind, confident that I was nothing but his lackey.

But I am not so willing to break ties with the

Bratva that I will cut out Sergei just yet. He's a disgusting man, but he has his uses.

He reached out to me, offering me a job as his bodyguard for the evening at a party at Seneca Lake, about five hours from our home in Brighton Beach. It's a luxurious countryside estate with a gorgeous view of the water, and the climate is perfect for the state's wine industry. The owner of this particular manor is one such winemaker — one who happens to have very close ties with the Bratva.

But as legitimate as his business is, a significant amount of smuggling takes place within those wine barrels, so nearly every smuggler and human trafficker worth their salt will be in attendance.

And it's one of those human traffickers who is my target for the evening.

Boris Mikhailov is his name. He's responsible for orchestrating the sale of hundreds of women from Serbia, Croatia, and Bosnia to powerful men here in the USA. He started out as the owner of some kind of loan shark operation that taught him the art of trapping trusting victims in need.

The only ones who will mourn his passing are the wastrels getting drunk on bad wine here this evening. And I have the perfect cover.

I arrive about fifteen minutes before Sergei, as arranged. I step out of my car, clad in a designer leather jacket and snug-fitting jeans that are flexible enough for easy movement. The tattoo of my

Russian star is just barely visible under the collar of my shirt.

I lean against my car, waiting for Sergei. It would be bad form for me to make an appearance without him, and I suspect he has this in mind — doesn't want me getting too far away from my place. All the better he's totally unaware that I'm using him as a cover for the night.

Some time passes as I check in with Cassie by text; she's been practicing her newfound painting talents while I'm "away on business." I often wonder how much she's guessed about the business I conduct. She knows I carry out some security jobs for the Bratva, and I've told her as much on this trip, but I've spoken not a word to her about the more...direct business I take care of.

Sergei's approaching sedan snaps me from my thoughts. He and his other muscle step out of the car; he's wearing a large fur coat and garish sunglasses, his patchy facial hair as unkempt and greasy as ever. He grins at me when he sees me approaching, but I know it's forced.

"Andrei, Andrei my boy!" He holds out his arms, and I embrace him out of courtesy.

"Safe trip, I hope?" I ask.

"Bah!" He gives a dismissive wave at his other bodyguard, the car's driver. "This *doorak* drives like a blind old man, but here we are, only an hour late,

155

eh?" He gives a cackling laugh and pats me on the back as the three of us head for the estate.

It's an opulent villa-style property, complete with fountains along the cobblestone walkway to the grand entrance and elaborate garden space out front — all patrolled by surly gentlemen carrying guns, of course.

The party is as boring as I expected it to be. Once we're inside, we're greeted by a manservant who guides us to a large room occupied by an array of middle-aged and older men every bit as sleazy-looking as Sergei. Each one of them has a scantily-clad young woman or two in their arms, and of course, wine is being shared freely among the guests. The women at these kinds of events are paid work-ers, though, not slaves, even if few of them look happy about tonight's gig.

It would kill the vibe of the party to show these flesh-peddlers the consequences of their business.

I'm surveying the crowd when I feel a tug at my arm as Sergei leans in to whisper to me. "Keep your manners in check tonight, Andrei, a few of the guests here haven't forgotten your reputation for, eh, 'bravado.' "

I arch my eyebrow at him, unfazed by the thinly-veiled threat. "You'd like that? I figured my bravado is why you keep hiring me for these things."

Sergei gives me a look, moving his lips as though swishing spit around in his foul mouth, and he's about to reply when he's cut off by another guest.

"Mister Slokavich!" comes a booming voice a small crowd of large men not far from where Sergei and I have entered. Sergei's face brightens up as he lays eyes on its source: a tall man in a relatively tasteful suit, relative to the rest of the people here, sporting a clean-cut beard and slicked black hair. Boris Mikhailov. My target.

"Boris, look at you, you bastard, it's been years!"

Sergei swiftly moves to meet him, greedily hugging him as anyone would embrace one of the richest men in the room.

"Aaah, you've lost weight, what are you, working out now?" Sergei's awkward compliments don't seem to bother Boris, who laughs it off easily. He's a shrewd talker.

"Well, a thriving business means more free time for that kind of thing, doesn't it? See, you're just too busy a man for all that," he jokes as he gives Sergei's pot belly a pat. The two of them laugh and greet each other properly, but I notice Boris's wolfish eyes glancing up at me periodically.

"And this man must have all the free time in the world," he says suddenly, gesturing toward me and beckoning me forward, "look at those muscles! Sergei, is this your prized *Shadow*?"

"Mine and mine alone," Sergei laughs, a hint of unease in his voice as I step forward with a smile.

"Is that indeed so?" Boris says, his question at Sergei but his eyes steadily on me. "Well, they do say such wolves tend to stray from their pack, don't they?"

There's a pause between us, and I know the phrase was a threat: my reputation for taking contracts outside the Bratva can't go secret forever, not in an environment like this. Nevertheless I only give a boyish grin. "Can't bring the pack the best prey without straying far, comrade."

Boris's face splits into a grin, and he points at me with a raise of his eyebrows to Sergei. "Look at this one, he's sharper than the rest of the muscle here, he is! Come, enough catching up, we have some important people to meet, and the wine is already flowing free."

The next hour or so passes with idle banter and light business talk. More relevant to me, Boris and Sergei seem inseparable. This lets me keep an easy eye on Boris, but I can't kill a man of his stature in front of Sergei without sealing my death sentence at a place like this.

So I keep the wine flowing, insisting that every passing server let us sample his wares. I've become rather good at pretending to drink, so as Boris and Sergei continue to indulge themselves, my head stays clear.

Eventually, we find ourselves wandering onto a

balcony overlooking the property, Sergei and Boris laughing at one of the latter's jokes.

"Sergei, my man, I can't tell you how disappointed I am we haven't worked together more," Boris says, wiping a tear from his eye. "Reminds me of old times when you and my father practically set up that operation in Hungary.

"Better times, my friend, better times," Sergei agrees, shaking his head.

"Ah," Boris suddenly says, his eyes falling on one of the serving women tending to another couple of men on the large balcony, "speaking of the Hungarian trade, you have yet to see some of my finest work. Ada! Get your luscious ass over here!"

The young woman who turns at Boris's command is beautiful, her long blonde hair spilling over one of her shoulders, and there's an unmistakable fear in her eyes as she makes her way over to Boris. "Yes, sir?"

"Sergei, this is Ada, one of my finest acquisitions, my jewel of the Carpathian basin," Boris introduces the woman, and I feel disgust boiling in my heart. Perhaps I was wrong about the nature of some of the women in attendance.

"Oh, indeed?" Sergei looks Ada up and down and licks his lips, obvious hunger in his eyes. "I suppose she has a wealthy client already, does she not?"

"She's been on standby to tend to the guest's needs

tonight," Boris replies, a devil's smile on his face. "I could tell you of how well she's been trained, but maybe it would be better for you to see for yourself, no?"

Sergei looks taken aback, but he chuckles with a disgusting grin to Boris as he takes the terrified Ada's hand. "You don't say? Well, I won't be one to turn down such a generous offer!"

Boris gives Ada a meaningful look, and she nods demurely, swallowing hard. "I believe our gracious host has guest rooms available for just such things," he remarks gesturing in a general direction, and without another word, Sergei takes Ada away, and I'm left alone with Boris.

After Sergei is out of sight, Boris turns his eyes on me, narrowing them as he takes a sip of his wine.

"You know, *Shadow*," he remarks, swirling his glass, "I've been trying to place why you look familiar.

I arch an eyebrow. Privately, I begin going through the names of men I've killed over the past few weeks, wondering if Boris might have known any of them particularly well — or rather, if word of my face might have gotten to him. "Oh?"

"Yes. There's something unforgettable about your jaw, the way the light catches it when you look over your shoulder." My muscles are already tensing, preparing to hurl this monster of a man over the balcony and make a run for it if need be; the client gave few specifications as to the manner of the man's death.

"You like gazing at my face in the moonlight, eh?" I shoot back with a smile, and Boris laughs.

"Not that way, my friend, but tell me…" He sets his glass down and crosses his arms, raising his chin and peering at me judiciously. "Where were you in '92?"

I blink and think for a moment before replying. "Hm. That year's a bit of a blur — I was in the middle of my sentence in prison, back in Siberia."

A spark of warmth comes back to Boris's eyes, and I see him roll up his sleeve to the forearm, showing me a black tattoo of a skull in front of part of a Russian star. A prison tattoo, unique to the prison where I served my time. My eyes widen in surprise, and without another word, the two of us embrace and exchange a greeting in Russian.

"Ha! And here I was thinking nobody here had seen as much hardship as me! Good you survived that hellhole, comrade," Boris says as we break apart, returning my smile.

"Impressive, just another thug from the world's blind spot running such a prosperous business as yours," I chuckle, nodding at him.

"Come, we have some *real* reminiscing to do. I know where our host keeps the good wine, out of the prying eyes of the rest of these fattened vultures."

Boris leads me outside the estate, a short walk to

the cellar entrance of the estate, a pair of large, fine oak doors leading to where most of the wine on the property was left to age.

It's cool and quiet inside as Boris leads me down, but our laughing chatter echoes through the rows and rows of fine barrels containing the best wine New York soil can produce — which isn't saying much, but coming from Siberia, I don't have the most refined palate for wine. Such things are for the leisure class.

"...and I remember, I remember seeing the guards drag him kicking from his cell after that little stunt of his, and they made him stand outside in the snow for the whole day! They nearly had to take off his legs from the frostbite!" Boris laughs at the memory, but our laughter is only part of how we cover up our inner scars from the abuses we suffered in prison. To this day, I've never known a greater hell.

Eventually we reach a cask obviously set up for sampling, a spigot already set up on a very low stool, the barrel coming up to our waists.

"Here," Boris beckons me closer, swaying a little as he tries to keep his balance, the wine strong in his blood, "this is where the owner is going to bring me and some of the richer guests later on — he'll try to impress them and say this is some of their fanciest stock, but it's only okay — and they won't miss a couple of glasses between brothers, will they?" He winks and fills our glasses, standing up and toasting with me as we drain them.

"Ah, but really, Andrei," Boris says. "You don't know what you're missing."

"What do you mean?"

"Working for the likes of Sergei, I mean," he says, looking meaningfully at me. "You won't get anywhere — New York is nice, but you're overquali-fied to be working for a man whose pride won't let him promote you any further than you are. He only cares for his own dynasty. You know he brought his bastard boy to the city?"

I arch an eyebrow in genuine surprise. "He has a son?"

Boris nods, a gossiping smile on his face. "His name's Kasym — Sergei knocked up some Chech-nyan daughter of a powerful man, and now Sergei's got to pay out the ass to pamper the boy. He's a little monster."

The memory of the rich young Chechnyan accompanying Sergei at the auction comes back to my mind, of the man that's currently looking for me — even if he doesn't yet know it's me — and my eyes widen. "I think I've seen the man. A monster, you say?" I keep a steady expression, but my heart skips a beat with worry.

"Horrible for business," Boris says in disgust, rolling his eyes. "Killed four of my girls in the few months he's been here. Can't control himself, I suppose — boys will be boys, no?" Boris laughs, but this time, my laugh along with him is feigned, anger roiling back up in my heart with renewed vigor. I haven't forgotten my job.

"Is nobody doing anything about the man?"

"Are you kidding?" Boris scoffs. "The man's grandfather is rich enough to buy this whole estate fifty times over, and his father is Sergei. Besides," he adds with an elbow to my arm, "those whores are a dime a dozen, just like the bitch Sergei is trying to shove his stubby little cock into right now. Who's going to mourn a few dead Hungarian cunts, anyway?"

"More than will mourn you."

Boris's glass is halfway to his lips when my fist catches him in the stomach like a piston. He nearly doubles over, the glass falling to the ground as he lets out a short, sharp groan, and before he can react, I grab hold of the back of his head and bring it crashing down into the top of the barrel, smashing his face through the wood and plunging it into the cheap wine within.

The human scum flails his arms, his mind probably still reeling to come to its bearings, totally caught off-guard. But my mind is as sharp and resolved as my muscles as my trunk-like arm holds his head under the liquid, solid and unmoving as a steel girder. My other arm wraps around him as I hold his arms to his sides. He's a strong man, thrashing as best as he can and giving me far more of a fight as the wine sloshes around him and some spills out onto the dirt, but he's no match for my sober strength.

After more time than a weaker man would have lasted, I finally feel Boris's body go limp, his lungs filled with the wine he was sampling just a few minutes ago.

The most inconvenient part of the job is the wine that now stains my jeans.

Wasting no time, I hoist up Boris's body, checking his now-still pulse before lifting his body over the top of the barrel and prying more of the wood off the top to make room before submerging his bulk into the barrel.

Much more of the wine spills onto the ground as I push him under the red liquid's surface. Carefully, I drag the barrel to a corner of stacked barrels, moving them around until I can place his new coffin towards the back, stacking a few barrels on atop the open upper side of Boris's barrel, effectively entombing him in wine casks.

I stand back to observe my work before looking down at my wine-soaked legs and sighing.

*Suppose it's an excuse to take Cassie on another shopping trip.*

I make my way back up to the manor — I still have a job to be at, after all. Sergei is probably finished with his deed by now.

Indeed, it doesn't take me long to find him making his way down one of the lavish hallways, past a few other drunken guests, Ada still under his arm, looking disgusted and downcast.

"Andrei, there you are!" His cheeks are rosy, obviously drunk beyond the point of wondering where I was. Exactly as I planned. "Andrei, you-you're the besht bodyguard in ALL THIS F-FUCKING PIGSTY," he howls, slinging half his drink onto the wall as he gestures wildly.

"Good to see you too, boss," I say, trying not to sound stiff.

"You know what, boy?" he laughs. "You, you take the rest of the night off, I'm going to find that other idiot to do this shit work. Thanksh to you, I'm gonna, I'm gonna be BEST pals with Boris, and his businessh is gonna have me ROLLING in cash! Here," he pushes Ada towards me, and I catch her gently, raising an eyebrow at him.

"Take this bitch, she wouldn't let me fucking touch her. Kick her ass for me, will you? Then you take the night off, go home to your, your little wife," he chuckles, and as he mutters something to himself, he staggers off, leaving me alone.

Ada looks up to me in fear, but I only put a finger to my lips. "Follow me," I say in a low voice.

Without saying a word, I guide the woman down to my car. Most of the party is too drunk to notice as we slip out, and once we're out in the night's air, Ada begins apologizing profusely to me.

"I'm sorry, I didn't mean to panic, but he was coming on like a mad dog, and after all the stories I've heard about his son, I —"

"You're going to be safe," I say firmly, and she's dumbfounded into silence for a moment.

"Wh-"

I help her into my car and get in on the driver's side, shutting the door and turning on the ignition. "Boris is dead. You'll never have to do that kind of work against your will again. Nor will you have to deal with Sergei again. I'm going to arrange a flight out of here for you — you can decide where you go, but New York won't be safe for you. Nor will the American west coast, for that matter."

She tries to form words, but her eyes are wide as her mouth just gapes, stunned at what she's hearing. I pull out of the driveway and start heading back towards the interstate.

"In the meantime," I say, pulling her seatbelt over her as we pull out onto the open road as I give her an even look, "I want you to tell me everything you know about Sergei's son, Kasym Slakovich."

CASSIE

*I*t's been a month since the wedding, and I've never been so happy in my life.

Andrei and I have spent most of our days jetting around the city, visiting museums, parks, theaters, restaurants, and even a couple live music venues. I am soaking up as much modern culture as possible, and my eyes have been wide and amazed nearly every waking minute. I had no idea how beautiful and diverse the world truly is, and I never thought I could feel this way… so immersed, so overwhelmed, yet completely exhilarated. There is still that voice in the back of my mind telling me that I will burn in hell for exposing myself to such temptation, for partaking in filth such as popular music and movies. But it's a softer voice now, more like a whisper, reminding me to remember where I came from and who I really am.

But the truth is, I'm not sure who I am anymore.

The things I have seen, the things I want now, are worlds apart from the sort of life I foresaw for myself even as recently as a month ago. The quiet, mundane, domestic lifestyle I aspired to my whole life now feels more like a death sentence in contrast to the exciting way I have been living lately. I am still constantly haunted by the spectre of my parents' expectations for me — screaming at me to be subservient and soft, to defer to my husband. And for the most part, I do. But it isn't out of fear or even a sense of godly duty. I want to follow his lead, because he has never led me into anything but joy and adventure. Andrei is my tour guide, my initiator. The man who keeps me on my toes and yet always makes me feel safe.

Despite my growing suspicions about what he does for a living.

He doesn't talk about it, and I don't ask, because I am terrified of bringing up something which might widen the slight rift between us. For as much as he appears to care for me, and as much as I definitely care for him, I do worry sometimes about the coldness he displays. Sometimes he is so incredibly soft, so gentle and warm, that it helps me forget the colder times. Many days we have spent together in the sunshine of mutual affection, Andrei showing me a whole new world, holding my hand all along the way. But then, there are so many nights when he slips away under the assumed cover of shadow, leaving me to awaken in the wee hours of an eerie dawn and find myself alone in the massive bed.

Early this morning, that's exactly what happened.

I woke up suddenly from a nightmare, instinctively turned on my side to snuggle into Andrei's warmth… only to realize that there was only a cold, empty place beside me. I was alone again, curled up tight in the dead silence of the apartment. Surely, it is a different kind of silence than what I was used to back home in upstate New York. Up there, the silence was complete — a total absence of sound. But here in the city, there was no such thing as complete quiet. There was always the muffled hum of neon signs, the bustle of traffic, wailing sirens and impatient car horns, even in the dead of night.

So this morning I lay there for hours, listening to the drone of city life down on the street, wondering which minutely small sound might just indicate the location of my husband. Where was he? What was he doing?

These questions plague me, keeping me from sleep. I watch the soft moon sinking down the sky on the other side of the curtains and worry incessantly about Andrei. I wanted some sign, some divine clue to tell me that at least he was okay. I need to know that he is safe, that he *will* come home again and rescue me from my anxiety.

When he finally returns, the sun is just beginning

to poke its luminous head from behind the horizon. I'm still lying in bed, and when I hear the quiet but distinct sound of the front door handle turning, I shut my eyes tightly and pull the blankets up to my face, pretending to be asleep. As desperately as I want to know what is going on, I am not quite ready to bring up that subject yet. It's just easier to pretend it isn't happening.

For now, at least.

When the bedroom door creaks open, I hear my husband step inside, his footsteps surprisingly soft considering his immense size and strength. He whispers, "Wake up, *printsessa*, I've brought you breakfast and tea."

I let out a little moan and yawn, slowly opening my eyes and sitting up in bed. I blink at him a couple times, pretending to struggle to wake up. I am a little ashamed of how good an actress I am, as Andrei adds, "Sleep well?"

Smiling, I give him a nod. He steps forward and sets a tray on my lap in bed, then puts a couple pastries and a paper to-go cup of hot tea on the tray.

"Good. Eat up. I'm going to shower."

He was always this curt and short with his words, but there was always a strange brusqueness to his tone when he returned from these random disappearances. He was distracted, his mind clearly in a different place. I wonder what he's thinking, what he's seen in the time he's been away from me.

"Th-thank you," I murmur, biting into a cherry pastry.

He hesitates for a moment on his way out, hanging on my words. He glances back over at me and even in the low light I can see a look of something like regret crossing his hard features. Like maybe he knows I know.

A little awkwardly, he gestures toward the tea and says, "Jasmine green tea with rosehips. Hope you like it."

Raising it to my lips and taking a scalding hot sip, I reply, "It's wonderful."

Andrei almost smiles for a moment, then simply nods and heads out of the room, leaving me alone yet again. I sit chewing my lip thoughtfully for a couple minutes, just staring down at the tray on my lap and wondering what I should do. I know it isn't my place to question my husband. I am his wife, and I must accept whatever he does or does not do with quiet humility and understanding. After all, I belong to him. I am just one small aspect of his life, one tool to make his life easier — not to interrogate him about what he does when he's not with me.

A horrible thought appears in the forefront of my mind: what if it's another woman?

But something tells me that can't be true; Andrei seems completely absorbed in our life together whenever he *is* with me. Surely if there was someone else, I would be able to tell. He would be distant, uncommunicative. At least, I assume I would know.

I want so badly to feel better about everything, to banish these dark suspicions and simply enjoy being with my husband again. After all, the vast majority of our time together is utterly blissful, even if I am still nervous and a little insecure around him. But he makes me feel cared for, taken care of, in a way I never dreamed possible. I sigh and set the tray aside carefully. Pulling my legs up to my chest, I let my chin rest on my knees as I sip my green tea and stare out the window. The sun is rising slowly, gradually bathing the Big Apple with morning light. I smile involuntarily, a sensation of fondness coming over me. I've really begun to love this city, despite its hidden dangers and pitfalls. Just like my husband.

I hear the squeak of the shower knobs being turned from across the apartment and then the comforting sound of the water pelting the walls and floors. I look down at myself. I'm wearing a lacy, powder-blue chiffon nightie and knee-high cream-colored socks, my hair plaited into braids over both shoulders. I have really learned to take some pride in expressing my spirit through my appearance. I suppose that makes me vain, and vanity is a mortal sin. But I can't help it — having someone like Andrei to remind me that I'm beautiful every day makes it difficult not to start liking myself a bit more. Back home, I never felt beautiful. I felt proper, decent, wholesome, well-presented, sometimes even pleasant-looking. But it was all about how thoroughly I could blend in with the rest of the women in the community. I had to wear the blandest clothes, the dullest colors, to numb my sex appeal and make me 'respectable.'

Over the past month, I have totally revamped my look to include bright colors, textures, prints, and styles I would have never even looked at back upstate. I know my wardrobe now would have me labeled a dirty Jezebel. A whore. A temptress.

But Andrei likes what I wear. And more importantly, as he'd encourage me to think: I like it.

I get out of bed and look at myself in the mirror across the bedroom, flicking on the light as I walk over. I look myself up and down, allowing my eyes to linger on the curve of my hip, the swell of my breasts. I never used to look at my naked body this way, seeing every inch of my flesh as dirty and unwholesome, an ugly thing to be covered with conservative clothing and hid away from the world. It is surprising to see that I like what's reflected in front of me.

Andrei has done so much for me, changing my entire perspective. I feel a sudden rush of appreciation and affection for him, and I immediately wish he was beside me so I could run to his arms and hold him close. Then it hits me: the overwhelming desire.

Something tingles all the way up from my toes to the top of my head. I have an idea.

I strip out of my nightie and socks, padding out of the room totally naked. To my surprise, the curtains across the massive living room window have been drawn, leaving me literally exposed before the whole city of New York. But instead of cowing me, of forcing me to hide, I feel strangely invigorated. I walk proudly into the bathroom, blinking in the steamy, aromatic fog. I am immediately enveloped by the warm, damp air.

"Andrei," I call out, fiddling with one of my braids a little nervously.

He looks over and does a double take, a flicker of desire passing through his dark eyes. His body is glistening under the hot stream of water, all sinewy muscle and taut flesh. I lick my lips without even thinking about it. I know exactly what I want — although I don't quite know how to do it. I want to make him feel as blissful as he makes me feel. In the past month we have had sex a few times, always gentle and slow, with Andrei treating me like a delicate object, something fragile which might shatter at any moment. He's made me come so many times with his skillful tongue and talented fingers, never demanding anything I didn't offer willingly.

I want to make him feel that way.

"Cassie," says my husband, leaning out of the stream of water to look at me more clearly.

"I have a question…" I begin, looking down at the stony floor, blushing.

"Yes?"

I look back up at him through a thick veil of eyelashes, biting my lip demurely.

"Can I join you?"

Andrei's eyebrows lift and he considers me for a moment, trying to determine whether I am being serious or not. But I am, one-hundred percent.

"Of course," he replies, moving over to make room for me. "Let me know if the water is too hot for you."

"Hot is good," I hear myself say. My heart pounding, I walk over and step into the shower stall, which is massive enough to hold far more than just two people. I slide in next to Andrei, who lets me stand under the water. I close my eyes and ease into the heat, sighing contentedly as the water warms my skin.

"What would you like to do today?" Andrei asks, and his tone betrays the fact that he is struggling to keep his voice even as it is thick with need.

I turn to him and hesitantly place my hands on his hard, muscular chest, looking up into his dark eyes. He blinks down at me in uncertainty, suddenly going almost rigid, as though paralyzed by my touch.

"You," I answer, shocked at my own audacity. It was such a filthy thing to say!

"Cassie…" he begins, his voice trailing off.

I press against him, the whole length of my body aligned with his. I can feel his manhood against my hip and thigh, starting to harden with just the slightest touch of my skin. The sensation gives me a heady confidence, as his shaft responds so positively to my movements. I lean in and press a soft, tender kiss into the center of his chest before letting my hand fall to the stiffening member between his strong thighs.

As my fingertips lightly graze its flushed crown, Andrei sucks in a sharp breath, obviously struggling to contain himself. I have never acted so boldly with him before, never taken the reins or the initiative in such a way. I know he is totally blindsided — and I like it.

"Do you want me to touch you there?" I purr, batting my eyelashes as I gaze longingly up into his eyes.

His lips part to allow a strangled, whispered, "Yes."

I gently wrap my fingers around his manhood and start to stroke it up and down, feeling the hot, silky skin smooth under my fingertips and palm. His size is still incredible to me, and I love the feeling of his massive length straining in my hand. He is so hard now, and I feel gratified in the knowledge that I made it this way.

As I stroke him a little tighter and faster, Andrei closes his eyes and leans slightly into my touch, licking his lips and moaning softly, his voice deep and gravelly. The low hum of his groans makes me wet in a place not even the shower water can reach. I want to make him feel so good — I have to show him how intensely I appreciate and crave him.

"Does that feel good?" I ask quietly, my own nipples stiffening as my breasts brush against my husband's strong chest.

"*Da, kotyonok*," he murmurs, nodding with his eyes closed in pleasure.

"I want to give you what you've given me," I tell him, standing on my tiptoes and kissing a slow, tantalizing trail along his collarbone.

Unable to resist any longer, I bend down to rest on my knees, looking up at Andrei to make sure he is okay with what I am planning to do. He's staring down at me with his dark eyes imploring, questioning now. But he doesn't tell me to stop. In fact, one of his hands comes down to stroke my head as I look up at him lovingly. Then he grabs one of my now-soaked braids and gently tugs on it, bringing my face closer to his crotch.

He wants it, too.

Uncertain but totally determined, I lean forward, close my eyes, and take his member in both my hands as I softly lick his crown. When I look up, Andrei is still watching me with his lips parted, breathing shallowly as though almost holding his breath, waiting for me to go on.

So I do.

Opening my mouth as wide as I can, I take as much of his massive shaft between my lips as possible, stretching my cheeks and letting my tongue flick along the underside of his member. I begin to suck him, bobbing slowly up and down on his shaft, groaning into the sensation of having yet another one of my orifices filled with my husband's glorious manhood. I am so wet now, my body clearly hungry to taste Andrei's seed, to swallow him down and feel him shudder with pleasure.

He cries out as I pump his shaft with both hands while my mouth sucks him in as deeply as I can manage, moving up and down with a quickening rhythm. I am surprised at how good I am at this, especially considering the fact that a month ago I would have gone pale with offense at the mere mention of this sex act. I can hardly believe how impetuous I'm being right now. How dirty I am. But… though I should be ashamed to admit it, I love this feeling.

I love knowing that I can bring such bliss to my handsome, powerful husband, causing such a strong and imposing man to tremble with the magic of my touch.

"Ohhh, *malyshka*, I'm almost there," Andrei moans. His hand starts to press more urgently at the back of my head, yanking my braid slightly in the process. This causes a minimal shock of pain which, instead of deterring me, only adds to my fervor. I am discovering that sometimes pain exists on a plane very, very near to pleasure.

I groan as my mouth sucks his shaft harder and faster, relaxing my throat to allow the head of his member to brush against the back of my throat. Even though my eyes water and I start to feel like I might gag, I refuse to relent — not when my husband is moaning and rocking into me with such authentic bliss. I can't stop now. I need to taste his seed on my tongue...

And with that, Andrei cries out and presses both hands against the back of my head, forcing me down on his shaft, hard. Just as I start to choke, I feel a hot, bitter spurt of come spill down my throat and I am forced to swallow it. He thrusts into my mouth a few times, his hands clawing at my hair, stroking the side of my face while he calls my name.

"Cassie! Oh, *printsessa!*"

When he finally releases me I stand up and look at him with rosy cheeks, hoping he will tell me how good I was, how well I performed.

He kisses me on the forehead and caresses my face fondly, peering into my eyes with genuine surprise and awe. "You are... a natural."

"I did good?"

Andrei nods and pulls me in for a kiss, and I wonder if he can taste himself in my mouth.

"I apologize for being a little rough toward the end. I lost control."

"I — I don't mind," I tell him, and it isn't a lie. Not in the least. I'm finding that I rather like being pushed to the limits. It makes me feel alive.

"Well, I hope you'll let me return the favor," Andrei says, reaching down between my legs to rub my slit. I gasp and collapse into his touch, letting him stroke me in his arms, bringing me to climax again and again, while the hot water slowly ran out.

\* \* \*

LATER THAT DAY, Andrei surprises me yet again, this time with tickets to a ballet.

We have spent the day in bed, exploring each other's bodies, drifting in and out of pleasurable, delicious sleep. We only took a break to eat a late brunch of pancakes and bacon, supplemented by homemade mimosas, which we brought back to bed with us. It's been another glorious day in my newfound marital paradise.

And now we are going to a *ballet*! I can hardly contain my excitement as we dress for the evening, both of us trying to look sharp and sophisticated for the kind of high-class crowd that attends such performances. He dresses in a navy blue suit and dark red tie, his black hair artfully tousled. I wear a sapphire-blue, satin dress that falls to my mid-calves. It has an embellished Peter Pan collar and pearly trim. I pair it with sparkling white tights and scarlet kitten heels, then twist my hair back into a fairly elaborate French braid.

Daring to be brave, I put on a small amount of mascara I picked out on a whim at a department store last week with Andrei, and find that I actually like the way it looks. My eyelashes are naturally quite thick, but since I am blonde, the tips of my lashes are nearly invisible unless you look closely. But with the pitch-black mascara, the entire length of my lashes is visible, and it gives me a glamorous, dramatic look befitting the ballet.

We head out to the show, find our seats, and when the curtain lifts, I immediately feel grateful that my mascara is waterproof. I am utterly, completely amazed by the beauty of the show. The costumes, the lighting, the orchestral music, the elegant and graceful movements of the dancers — all of it is entrancing and bewitching in a way I've never experienced.

I find myself longing to dance that way, to feel my limbs flex and stretch into beautiful curves and lines. I want to be lifted and carried by the music, to become a moving, living embodiment of art and grace. I cannot believe that my parents, my doctrine, ever insisted to me that something so beautiful could be sinful.

Tears streak down my face throughout the entire

four-hour performance, and unlike at the opera, Andrei remains at my side the entire time, holding my hand. After the final curtain closes and we head back out into the cold New York City night, he turns to me and asks what I think.

"It was beautiful," I gush, leaning on him and wiping at my eye gingerly.

"You were crying. Are you alright?" he asks, stroking my hair. His face remains hard, but his voice is tinged with just the sweetest hint of softness.

"I just… I have never seen something so amazing in my whole life, Andrei. I never knew how moving it could be to see something like that. I can only imagine how much more wonderful it must be to dance the way they do. I wish I could."

Andrei stops suddenly, causing me to look up at him quizzically.

"What is it?" I ask, cocking my head to the side.

"I think I know someone who can teach you."

## ANDREI

"*Y*ou just hold your shoulders like so, keep all the tension away — it will only hold you back. There, that's good, lovely! You'll be sliding across the dance floor like water in no time."

Sonya stands back and lets Cassie go through the short routine she's been practicing all week once again. Both of them are happier than I've seen them in a long time.

I made sure that Sonya had a place of her own to start teaching ballet on her own terms. It's a quaint but very classy place in SoHo, downstairs from her new apartment. I used the money her mother paid for the hit to pay for it, calling it a favor for an old friend. There was a little publicity in the high culture community over her late coach's murder, but that only seems to have helped her get her studio up and running successfully.

Cassie, meanwhile, has been flourishing beyond her expectations. Her moves are still unrefined, but she has the natural grace of a bird, her body becoming more used to the fluid motions with every passing day she trains.

And the look on her face when she moves so freely makes it worth all the work that's brought us to this point.

I sit near the door as I watch her finish her lessons to the gentle, elegant music. The two of them are totally enraptured in the activity; I made sure to pay Sonya for private sessions.

As the lesson comes to an end, Cassie turns her attention to me, and her face brightens up even more than it was before. With the grace of a gazelle, she bounds over to me and throws her arms around me, and I lift her up to a delighted giggle.

"I didn't even realize you were there, you're too sneaky!" she said as I planted a kiss on her cheek. "Sonya says I'm making leaps and bounds! I mean, I am literally, but you know what I mean."

"Of course," I laugh back as I set her down. "You seem like you were born to do this, the way I see it. I can't wait to see you in a performance of your own, before long."

Cassie's cheeks go pink, and she beams up at me, embarrassed. "I don't know about *that*, I'm only just getting my body used to the kind of flexibility this stuff takes. I can't imagine how Sonya's gotten as talented as she is."

Cassie's instructor gives me a wave from across the room on her way into the office, and I return it with a smile. We haven't spoken much since her getting set up here, but I hear about her appreciation through Cassie.

Sometimes I wonder whether she suspects anything about my involvement in everything that's changed in her life over the past few weeks, but I try not to think too far into it. I'm already following up on one person linked to a past target; I can't keep up a network of them.

"A lot of training," I say simply, "but she will be the first to tell you that a well-deserved rest is just as important. Come on," I say, suddenly reaching down and sweeping her off her feet. She yelps and throws her arms around my neck, curling up into my embrace as I head out the door and start walking towards my car. "Your legs must be awfully tired, so it's only right that I give you a lift home, don't you think?"

* * *

BACK AT HOME, I push open the door to our room as Cassie's lips press into mine, and my hand squeezes her ass as I draw her closer into me, my manhood hard against her as she grinds up against me needfully.

I lift her up and toss her onto the bed, and she lands gracefully, rolling onto the sheets and spreading her limbs with a satisfying stretch as she rubs her body into the soft mattress.

All around the walls of our room are pieces of Cassie's artwork, hung up on display. Canvases large and small adorn nearly every corner of the room, and the ones hanging up are only the ones Cassie was really happy with. She's been incredibly prolific, using nearly every hour she isn't dancing at the easel.

I don't pretend to have an eye for art, but to my perspective, she seems to be getting better every day.

Having lived so minimalistically for so long, the jolt of color in the room is something I'm still getting used to, but the more time I spend around it, the more I think I appreciate it. There's something to be admired in surrounding yourself in the work of your own hands — or those of someone close to you, in my case.

I step closer to the bed, stripping my shirt and shoes off before putting a knee beside her and looming over her with a hungry smile. She flutters her eyes back up to me, biting her lip as she twirls a lock of her hair around a finger. There's something in her eyes I can't quite read, but my lust is getting the better of me as she toys with her bra strap, the gentle, subtle motions of her body on the bed just begging me to rip her clothes off her.

So my hands go to her dress, nearly tearing the fabric as I rip it off her, exposing her lithe and limber body, her breathing getting faster as she turns her neck up to me. I dive in for her as if on instinct, sucking at the sensitive flesh with abandon.

"Please, *solnyshko moyo*," I hear her whisper, "please, I want to feel you all over me!"

I pause, moving my face up to hers as a grin spreads across my face unbidden. I take her chin in my thumb and forefinger and raise an eyebrow at her as her hands run up and down my hardened abs.

"*Solnyshko moyo*? I never thought myself very much like 'sunshine,' but I'll take it. Where did you learn that one?"

Cassie turns her head into her shoulder bashfully. "Well, I asked Sonya to teach me a little Russian in our downtime, and that one was, well, I don't know, I like the way it sounds."

My grin widens, and I lean forward to kiss her, the warmth of our lips pressing together making my heart beat faster, and my strong hands grip her sides lovingly as I press the bulge of my manhood up against her before rolling onto the bed beside her.

"The two of you seem to be getting along rather well, no?"

"She's nice," Cassie answers, her eyes sparkling as she smiles at me, her face framed by the cascade of her blonde hair. "We've gone out into town a few times together, and we text some. I don't think she's very used to having people to hang out with, but I don't either, besides you, and I think that kind of makes it easier for the two of us to feel comfortable around each other, you know?"

"It's good to have someone to relate to," I agree.

"It's funny," Cassie adds with a smile, "she's almost a whole year younger than me, but the way she acts, she comes off almost like an older sister. I like her."

"I'm glad," I say, wrapping my arms around her and bringing her in close, pressing my lips to her forehead. "There doesn't seem to be anything you can't adapt to, *printsessa.*"

"Mmhmm," she murmurs, and as she does, something seems a little 'off' about the look in her eyes. I pause and tilt my head, peering at her searchingly.

"What's the matter? Something seems to be on your mind."

Cassie opens her mouth and closes it again almost immediately, her face getting some color to it, and within a few seconds, she's blushing furiously as she struggles to find her words.

"I don't think anything's wrong, it's just…"

I sit up in the bed, looking a little concerned now. "Are you wanting for anything? Don't be afraid to speak your mind, Cassie, you know that by now."

"It isn't that," she says, twirling some bedsheet

around her finger. "It's just... I'm...I'm a few weeks late, Andrei."

I feel my heart skip a beat, and my eyes widen as I look into hers. "Cassie…"

"I didn't think much of it at first," she goes on, biting her lip. I can tell that every word is riddled with fear, and I reach out to take her hand, reassuringly. "But the other day when I was out with Sonya, I...I asked to stop by a corner store and pick up a test. You know, just to be safe."

I'm hanging on to every word now, leaning in and holding Cassie's hand close to me. There's a long, terribly long pause as she stares down before she lifts her eyes to meet mine, a small, hopeful smile appearing on her lips.

"Andrei, I'm pregnant."

The feeling welling up in my chest is completely and utterly new and overwhelming.

Joy.

Without another moment, I wrap my hands around Cassie's back and lift her up into a deep kiss, and then another, and another, peppering her face and neck with kisses until she giggles and squirms under me.

I can feel her relief like a lead weight off her shoulder, and she throws her arms around my neck to return my kisses as we roll on the bed together.

"Cassie, that's — that's wonderful!"

"Oh god, Andrei," she breathes as she buries her

face into my chest, and her eyelashes tickle my pecs, "I've never been so happy!"

I lick my lips as I stare at her, something stirring in me I was unfamiliar with before today — a new passion that seems to make Cassie glow like more radiant an angel than the first day I saw her. "Cassie, I don't know what to do with how I feel," I nearly lose my grasp of English as I find myself laughing, giddy, "but there's nobody else in the world I'd rather share this indescribable feeling with. This is amazing, Cassie."

Her beautiful mouth spreads into a grin, and the new passion within me drives me down onto her, gently, pressing my lips to hers and delving my tongue into her mouth, reveling in her while our bodies grind together on the bed.

"I've never been prepared to handle this kind of thing," Cassie whispers, "I mean, I've always known it would happen, but I never learned..."

"There will be time for that," I answer, wrapping her in my arms and squeezing her tight, "for now, we should just be happy. Something that's *yours* is growing inside you. Something that's *ours*. Something we made as one."

A short, hot breath escapes Cassie as I press my manhood against her, and my hands around her back unhook her bra, tossing it aside and letting her breasts spill out.

I bring my hands up her back and massage the

tense, exhausted muscles bound up behind her, and she rolls her neck around as I manipulate her as if she were a ragdoll. My hands work her muscles deftly, wanting her relaxed and open for when I take her.

"You," she breathes as she turns her neck up to me, exposing herself as my victim, my prey, "you put this in me. You gave me part of you. We made all this," she says as she strokes my sides, rippling with abs, and her doe eyes stare up into mine with utterly helpless desire. "I'm all yours."

"I know."

My mouth goes to her exposed, stiff nipple as my fingers go to her cunt, slipping under the elastic of her underwear and finding that slick slit as if it were made for my hand. As my tongue lashes out to stroke the surface of the areola, torturing the needful, swollen tip, my fingers stroke at the swollen nub between her legs, wasting no time with idle play.

Cassie is mine, and I'm going to make her feel so.

"Aaah!" Cassie yelps as my fingers move aggressively down into her needy pussy, and my fingers start moving further and harder into her, stroking the inner walls of her pussy while my thumb rubs at her clit. I can feel her body squirming under me as I take her in three different spots. She doesn't know how to react to such an overwhelming sensation.

My teeth graze her nipples as I suck at her tits, and she starts to turn her body as if to recoil, but then I give a long, hard stroke of my fingers along the upper walls of her womanhood, and her stomach clenches and her hands grasp at the sheets. But then her clit also feels my onslaught, and with my fingers controlling her from her depths, it has even less means of escape. She's totally and utterly mine.

"Oh, Andrei," she whimpers. "Oh! Ohhh!"

The rhythm of my fingers is unrelenting, and it isn't long before I feel her orgasm cresting. "Andrei, Andrei it's so much, I can't..." she manages, her eyes unfocused as the sensation overwhelms her. Then I feel her stomach start to clench as she nears the point of no return.

Just when I see her eyes shut tight, and I can feel her start to climax, I withdraw my fingers and raise my head, kissing her deeply as I feel her whole body shake under me in protest, trembling at being denied what it was so close to, so desperate to have.

"You carry our child, *printsessa*," I say to her as I break our kiss, "you will experience my body in its entirety."

As I finish the sentence, I'm already helping her nearly-limp body out of her underwear, and my own soon follows, freeing my cock and letting its girth present itself before Cassie.

She's nearly panting, desperate with desire for my body, for a taste of all of me, and almost immediately, she crawls on her knees towards me, her hands going to my cock to bring her hungry lips to my crown.

"No, darling, not tonight," I say as I hold her, running a hand through her golden hair as her watery eyes look up at me. "Tonight, you get only the best of me — only more of what I've already given you."

I guide her up as I sit back, my shaft standing straight up and erect like a terrible spear, and I guide Cassie up as she readies her womanhood to be impaled by it.

"Do you want to give yourself to me?" I ask her as she bites her lip, cautiously but eagerly bringing her pussy to my bulging crown. It stiffens even more as the two organs make contact, and the shudder that escapes Cassie's lips gives me my answer.

"Yes, Andrei, please," I hear her pronounce carefully in breathy, needy Russian, "I want to give my all."

A grin spreads across my face, and I reach up to her hips, giving them a gentle tug to start to lower her body onto my spear. "Then come to me, *printsessa*."

Her eyes widen in anticipation and fear as I start to pull her further onto my shaft, and I see her eyes watching it, knowing that I'm going to stuff all of it up into her. Her narrow hips look almost unable to hold it all, even as one of her delicate fingers toys with her clit as I hold her up there atop my scepter.

I give her another tug, and she bites her lip, uncertain. "Are you sure it will…?"

"I'll be right here with you, Cassie," I whisper back, and with a cautious nod, she lets herself relax, and I pull her all the way down my shaft.

Immediately, her sharp cry pierces the room as she falls upon my hardened cock down to the hilt, warming her insides as my rod swells and throbs within her.

I start bucking up, rocking her around me as if she were as light as paper as my cock throbs, and she struggles to keep her hands somewhere solid as she moves around. The thought of Cassie bearing my child, holding within her something that a person as angelic as her has created with me, it fills me with a passion I never knew, and my cock feels harder and larger than ever before.

I'm merciless, bucking up and rocking Cassie around with the same relentless rhythm I was fingering her with a few minutes ago.

"Oh, ohhh," Cassie moans as I feel her tightening under me, but I will not be so cruel as to keep her waiting any longer — I thrust up into her, my cock swelling and rubbing every inch of her insides, and she cries out "Andrei!" as her honey floods around me, but I don't even think about ceasing. My hardened abs lift my manhood up and into her over and over again, like a machine in its rhythm and energy.

The very air around us feels charged as her

warmth fuels my cock, the same energy that created the child we'll soon share.

"Cassie," I breathe out in a husk, "I've never felt anything like you before. Fuck, for a pristine angel," I say as I lift and hold her up on my cock as her head rolls around, hardly aware in the haze of ecstasy, "you're ruining me."

I'm practically using her like a cocksleeve at this point, watching her orgasms roll in as her eyes clench or a whimper escapes her, and my dick is absolutely soaking in her juices. But even as she douses me, the fire inside me only grows fiercer, and my shaft goes harder than ever before as I feel my climax roaring forward.

I've already been holding her up, but I pull her deeper onto me now, and her body clenches even tighter as I pump more and more fiercely as my rhythm starts to slip away and fall apart.

Finally, my jaw hangs open and my voice roars out as my fire bursts into her, shooting up into her womanhood harder and in greater volume than ever before in all my time with Cassie, and the bliss on her face is indescribable.

The jets of my come coat her insides, her pussy tight around me, and even as I fill her up completely and utterly, emptying myself into her, I realize I've never been closer to another human being than now. I feel a warmth in my heart, burning hotter with each throb of my manhood as she tightens around me, and slowly, I let her sink down on top of me while I'm still inside her, our arms wrapping around each other's bodies as we help each other descend from our orgasms.

Finally, the draining of my cock comes to an end, and we're left with our foreheads pressed against each other, one of my fingers playing with her hair as she strokes my glistening chest, both our breaths coming out long and easy.

I feel her gazing at me, and I lean in to kiss her gently on the lips, running my free hand up and down her. Her body is nearly trembling it's so overexerted, but pressed up next to me, she feels so secure that she could fall asleep.

"I had no idea what to expect from you when we met, Andrei," she whispers, "but now, I'm looking at one of the happiest moments of my life."

It's a few moments before I reply.

"I never thought I'd be able to say the same...yet here I am." I turn to her and smile, and the one she gives me back melts my heart all over again.

"I can't wait to see this child come into this world, Cassie," I whisper. "I'll give it everything I can in this harsh world."

"It's a boy," Cassie whispers back, and I blink, peering at her.

"How do you know?"

"Just do," she says with a tilt of her head.

I watch her for a moment, then chuckle and feel

giddy, my mind swimming with thoughts. "I suppose we'll have to decide on a name — and whether it will be an American or Russian one."

"I'm open to ideas," she says with a grin, then closes her eyes and cuddles into me.

My chest moves up and down slowly, and I'm about to drift into a light doze when her voice reaches my ears again and snaps me back to attention.

"I can't wait to tell my parents."

## CASSIE

*J* stare down at the cell phone in my lap, the fancy new iPhone I've hardly used since Andrei bought it for me a month ago. I've never had my own phone before, and I generally only used it to look things up and play games. But now, holding it in my trembling hand, there is a truly serious call I needed to make.

It's time to contact my parents.

Ever since the wedding, I've had to push them out of my mind just to get through. Being with Andrei nearly every waking hour has certainly helped assuage my homesickness, as well as distract me from my conflicted emotions regarding my mother and father and what they did to me. At first, they were constantly on my mind, their stern voices scolding me and shaming me for everything I did. But over time, their influence over me has waned, and I've started to finally feel more independent — like my decisions are finally mine to make. I've had to grow up fast, after eighteen years of living in a conservative vacuum with my insular community.

And now I'm making a huge leap into full adulthood, taking on the ultimate responsibility: motherhood. Butterflies flit around in my gut just thinking about it. Curled up on the couch in the living room, I look up out of the huge window to watch the sun starting its slow descent toward the peach-pink horizon. I smile nervously to myself and rub my hand over my stomach, trying to wrap my mind around the fact that there is a tiny flicker of life growing inside.

I've got to call them. I need to. I'm having their first grandchild! Surely they will be ecstatic to hear this news. I can't imagine them reacting negatively to something so pure and beautiful as a new baby. After all, as a woman of God, it is one of my primary duties in life to have kids. Surely they'll appreciate that.

Even if they disapprove of everything else. But… I don't have to give them *all* the details, do I? They don't *need* to know what all I've been up to since they married me off to a big, strong, mysterious stranger. But they do need to know that I'm having a baby with him!

My heart hammers in my chest and I bite my lip anxiously as I slide the phone screen open and click on the call icon. I dial my parents' phone number, the only number I've ever memorized besides 911, then hesitate before pressing "CALL." My thumb hovers over the button for a full ten seconds while I start to reconsider. What if they ask too many questions? What if they are disappointed in me?

No, I tell myself firmly. They love me. And they will love this baby, too.

With that warm thought, I smile to myself and confidently press the call button, lifting the phone to my ear. I listen to the ticking sound of my phone trying to connect, my heartbeat at a galloping pace by now. I wonder who will pick up the phone? It's a home line, and part of me hopes that Isaiah beats them to the phone so I can finally hear his voice again. My soul aches for such a sweet, familiar voice.

After a couple seconds, I scowl at the phone, wondering when it's going to start ringing. Perhaps I just don't get very good service in this particular spot, I think to myself. So I get up and walk into the bedroom, pacing while the line still attempts to connect.

Finally, there is a pause… and then a loud BEEP-BEEP-BEEP.

A female voice says, "We're sorry. Your phone call could not be completed as dialed. This number has been disconnected. Please check to make sure you have dialed the correct number and try again." Then there's a final beep and the line goes quiet, the call ended.

My blood runs cold, but I refuse to believe it. I check the number, make sure I typed it in correctly, then press "call" again. I bite my nails as I pace back and forth in the bedroom, getting impatient as the phone tries once again to connect, only to receive the same error message.

This can't be happening. They couldn't have changed their number. Not without telling me — of course not! I'm their only daughter! I'm their child! There's no way they would do something like this without warning me, without giving me the new number. Besides, they have had the same house phone number since before I was even born. It makes no sense that it would be disconnected now, after all these years, unless…

They did it on purpose.

To sever ties with me. To keep me out of their lives.

"No, no, no!" I mumble to myself, tears forming in my eyes and panic starting to take hold of me. "This can't be happening. Something is wrong."

I toss my iPhone onto the bed as though it's covered in barbs, as though it's something poisonous. I can't look at it right now. I can't deal with this. I thought I would be crying happy tears as I told my parents that they'll be expecting a grandchild, not shedding angry, bitter tears at the thought of being abandoned by my own parents! I look around instinctively for Andrei, my safety blanket, my comfort, my shelter from the emotional storm brewing in my heart.

But he isn't here. I forgot. He's at the apartment gym complex downstairs, working out as is his evening routine. I catch a glimpse of myself in the mirror across the room — my pink-rimmed eyes, my blotchy cheeks, my messy hair, and slouchy comfy clothes. I look like a disaster. But I am a disaster in need of my husband.

So I quickly throw on a wraparound sweater and slip-on shoes before rushing out into the hallway, nearly running to the elevator. I'm trying to hold myself together so that anyone who sees me on my way to the gym won't think I'm a crazy person in mid-meltdown.

Even though I am. And I am not holding it together well at all.

I race through the lobby to the gym, fiddling with the door — only to remember that I need a key to get in. I stand on tiptoe to look through the small, square glass window in the door. I can see Andrei lifting weights across the room, looking totally absorbed in the activity, his eyes intense and determined. I jiggle the doorknob in vain, tears welling up in full force at this point. Finally, I get so frenzied and upset that I start pounding on the door with my tiny fists, hoping to make enough noise to catch Andrei's attention.

It takes about half a minute for him to break out of his work-out trance and notice me banging on the gym door. His eyebrows shoot up in surprise as he jogs over to let me in, his hard body glistening with sweat.

"What's the matter, *malyshka*?" he asks, voice filled with genuine concern as he takes both my hands.

Tears pulse down my cheeks as I look up at him, struggling to find the words.

"My-my parents… I tried to call them, but I-I couldn't g-get an answer! The lady says th-the number has been d-disconnected!" I whimper, feeling my lip tremble.

Suddenly, a look of dark comprehension comes over Andrei's sharp features and he looks more wolf-like than ever before. He looks like a predator — an alpha animal.

"I assumed that might be the case," he says in an undertone, shaking his head. I can tell that he is gritting his teeth, his hands releasing mine and subtly clenching into fists at his sides.

"What d-do you mean?" I ask, squinting up at him. What a strange thing to say.

"I had a feeling this would happen," he begins cryptically, scowling at the floor with his arms across his chest. "Cassie, please don't let this bother you."

I shake my head and back away from him slowly a few steps. "What are you t-talking about? Of course this bothers me! I need to get in contact with m-my parents! They need to know I'm p-pregnant!" I sob, tears dampening my shirt.

Andrei gives me the most pitying look in the world, and suddenly I feel irrationally angry with him. Why isn't he helping me? Why is he reacting this way? He steps toward me, opening his arms as though to embrace me, but I refuse to let him just gloss over this. It is a big deal!

"I need help, Andrei! We've g-got to look them up and get their new number. What if s-something happened to them? I can't just let this go."

He sighs heavily. "I should have warned you this might happen. I need to be honest with you, *printsessa*. Please listen to what I tell you. *Moya lyubov*, your mother and father are not good people. They sold you like you were cattle."

Indignant fury bursts like a firework in my chest.

"And you bought me! Doesn't make you any better, does it?" I shout at him.

He goes quite pale in the face and his expression is so dour, so dark, that for a moment I actually fear what he might do to me for saying that. But it isn't the fear of what he'd do to me. Not really. It's the fear of what my father would have done to me, manifested in my husband, the only other man I've ever been close to.

But he is not my father. Instead of lashing out or hurting me, he swallows hard, lets his arms fall to his sides, and says softly, "I was only there to work security. I did not go there with the intention of buying a wife." His voice is tinged with a bit of sadness, but I'm too upset to let it drop.

"B-but you did! You bought me! You took me away from my f-family and brought me here and now you won't help me get in touch with them. Wh-why are you hurting me like this?" I cry, rushing forward to helplessly, harmlessly beat his chest with my fists.

"Cassie! They have abandoned you because they're ashamed of what they've done to you, of what your father's greed has done to you. They cannot tell anyone the truth. Think of what a scandal it would be: Arnold Meadows, with his beautiful house and perfect family — selling his only daughter to get out of debt!" Andrei hisses through gritted teeth.

"No! That's not true!" I cry, shaking my head, feeling sick to my stomach.

"It *is* true! They mistreated you terribly, *sladkaya*. I cannot change the past, and neither can you. Cassie, you did nothing wrong. You didn't deserve what *etot ublyudok* did to you. I want so badly to help you, to make you feel better, but you have to know that I cannot bring you back to them. They don't want you anymore — think of how easily they threw you away, put you on display, for sale! You don't need them, *malyshka*. You are better than that."

I am stunned at his words, tears streaming down my face. My heart is so heavy, so full of pain at the prospect that Andrei may be right. And deep down, way deep inside my heart, I know it is true. They have not even tried to contact me. Since the wedding, it's been like I don't even exist in their universe anymore.

They really have left me behind.

I will never see my parents again. Nor will I get to hold Isaiah in my arms. He will never get to meet his little nephew. I feel so broken, like a part of my soul has died.

"It hurts, Andrei," I weep, my shoulders shaking as I sink into his arms as though totally deflated. "I can't believe it... they never even loved me, did they?"

His arms wrap around me, stroking my hair, rubbing my back as I sob into his hard, shirtless chest. "Oh, *dorogaya*, I don't know. I'm sure they did, in their own way."

"I've lost my whole family. I'm all alone," I sob.

"No, no, no. You are not alone," he says, holding me back and taking my chin in between his fingers to tilt my face up. His dark eyes, usually so cold, are warm — blazing with love. "You will never be alone again. I am *vasha sem'ya* now. We will be a family together: you, me, and the little one growing inside you. And I promise our life together will be so bright that it will outshine the pain of what you've lost. I promise you that. *Obeshchayu.* I swear."

Suddenly, it all makes sense. This is what God has planned for me.

It has been a dark, treacherous path that led me here and I have lost so much in the process, but I know now, in this instant, that this is exactly where I am meant to be. It doesn't matter much *where* I am, only that I am with Andrei, my prince charming. And that ever since I've met him, he's never hurt me. Never done a thing to make me feel unwelcome or scared, despite his secrets. He's only ever encouraged me to do the things I enjoy, and my self-confidence and happiness has blossomed with him at my side.

"I love you."

The words fall from my lips before my brain can even process them.

Andrei's eyes widen and then, slowly a brilliant smile appears on his face. He looks so immensely relieved, so happy, and the joy in his face makes him practically radiant.

"*Ya tozhe tebya lyublyu.* I love you, too."

I throw my arms around him and he kisses me, his hands smoothing away my tears, brushing the hair back out of my face, caressing my shoulders, my arms, all the way down my back. I lean into him fully, my lips parting to dive my tongue into his mouth. He kisses me deeply, passionately. His hard body, still glistening slightly with a sheen of sweat, is so tempting, so beautiful. I cannot resist him, nor do I want to.

We are each other's family now, forever. And I need him, now.

He hoists me up, my legs wrapping around his waist instinctively. His lips and mine move together as he carries me across the gym, never breaking our kiss except to occasionally come up for air. Andrei carries me through a door into a wooden room in the back. The warm, wet heat trickles into my sensory recognition, and it dawns on me that we're in the gym sauna.

He sits down on a wooden bench along the wall with me still straddling him. His lips break away from mine to follow a passionate, intense trail down my neck, sucking dark red blooms under my skin while I moan with pleasure. The sensation is ticklish and sweet and ever so slightly bordering on pain. I start to undulate my hips, rolling against the growing bulge at the front of his pants. I want him inside me now, now, now. I need him to fill me up and make me feel complete. I need to feel connected with him, our bodies as close as possible.

"I love you so much," I murmur against his skin, breathing him in.

Andrei peels my shirt up over my head and tosses it, leaving my chest, back, and shoulders exposed to the balmy atmosphere. *"Moya printsessa,"* he growls, his lips moving down to lightly suck my nipple. My private parts respond with a tingling pleasure as I start to ache for more, needing to feel him inside me.

As he licks and gently bites my nipples I arch my back and shut my eyes, moaning. It is amazing to me how his mouth on my breasts elicits such a strong response from a totally separate part of my body. It must be magic, I think. It must be some kind of power.

"I need you, Andrei," I sigh, shuffling off of his lap to strip out of my pants and underwear. Suddenly I am distinctly aware of the fact that we're in a public place. Someone could walk into this sauna and see me completely naked at any moment. For Cassandra Meadows, this would have been absolutely unimaginable. Totally impossible.

But for Cassandra Petrov, this is exciting.

In fact, the knowledge that we could be discovered any second now only spurs my desire.

Andrei quickly slips out of his workout pants and shoes before standing up to kiss me again, his arms wrapping around me and tugging me close. His hands wander down to cup my ass, his fingers sliding around my hips to toy with my slit. My surprised, blissful cry is swallowed into Andrei's mouth as he kisses me, his fingers working their way inside of me while his thumb circles that tight little bundle of nerves at the crown of my privates.

I can't help but rock into his touch, my body responding with involuntary enthusiasm to the spirals of pleasure radiating upward from between my legs. His fingers and thumb work their magic, moving rhythmically as Andrei's lips trail down my neck, leaving a path of bruising kisses on the way. I can feel my pleasure mounting higher and higher until finally I collapse in his arms as my first climax shudders through my body.

"Ohh my goodness!" I whimper breathlessly.

Andrei's arms have to support me for a few minutes while we stand there kissing, as my legs are so shaky and weak from my overwhelming release. But as I regain my strength, my desire intensifies. I reach down between us to wrap my fingers around Andrei's thick shaft, reveling in its smooth, rock-hard length. I pump him up and down, fast and hard, as his breath comes heavily. He kisses me aggressively, biting my lip, while his hands squeeze my backside and claw their way up my back to tangle in my hair. I can tell he is losing control — becoming more animalistic, less gentlemanly.

Instead of being afraid or put off by this change, I find myself panting with need. I want him to take me, to use me and mark me as his own. He is my family now, and I want more than anything to feel united with him, with his hard, hot flesh. I want him to be rough, to use me however he pleases, so long as he is mine and I am his.

"Andrei," I breathe, "I want you to take me. Please."

His chest is heaving as he looks down at me through heavily-lidded eyes, his lips parted. I am suddenly fully aware yet again of just how massive, how muscular and imposing my husband is. I know that he could break me in half without even trying. If he were to let go, his usually gentle touches could become aggressive, even dangerous. I can tell that he is struggling to contain himself, fighting with some primal need to tear me apart, to use my body in a way that might actually hurt me.

And I long for him to give into it.

"Please. Take me however you want. You don't have to be gentle anymore. I'm ready."

I tell him this emphatically, though my voice still trembles.

"*Ya ne mogu*. I don't want to hurt you, Cassie," he replies, his jaw clenching. I know he wants this, too, and he is on the brink of losing the tightly-held control he's been clinging to ever since we first made love. I realize that he has had to work so hard to please me, to love me without hurting me, and a rush of warm affection comes over me.

"I don't mind," I answer, my hand still stroking his shaft. "Please, I want you to lose control, Andrei. I want you to… to *fuck* me like you really want to."

I've never said that word before. I've never even *thought* that word before. But Andrei's eyes go wide and blazing and I know immediately it must be setting him off. He knows now that I'm serious, that I really and truly want him to let go and finally take me with abandon.

And he does.

Without wasting another second, Andrei picks me up and spins me around to face the wooden bench, his hands pushing on my back to bend me over. I brace my hands on the wooden bench and look back behind me to see Andrei positioning the head of his member at my wet entrance. The steamy air of the sauna fills my lungs as I inhale sharply, my body shuddering at the slightest touch of his shaft to my aching slit. He's going to take me from behind.

One of his hands roves up my back to grab my hair, pulling my head back. I let out a little yelp of surprise, my private parts responding to this show of dominance with a tingling approval. I want to be completely submissive to him in this moment — I want to give him absolutely anything and everything he's ever wanted.

"Say you want it," Andrei growls, rubbing the head of his manhood up and down my slit.

He gives my hair a little tug and I respond, "I want it, oh please."

And with that, he pushes inside of me, filling me up until I can feel his tip hitting that deep, secret spot. At this angle, he is able to hit that impossibly delicious spot so easily! I moan as he starts to pound into me mercilessly, his massive shaft sliding in and out of me so fast and hard that I see stars. He smacks my backside and I cry out in mingled pain and pleasure, wanting more, always more.

"Yes! I want it — I want it to hurt!" I manage to choke out between heavy breaths.

Andrei responds with another hard slap, and then he grabs hold of my hips with both hands, using this position to slam into me with more power and precision. I suddenly feel another climax coming, and when it does I cry out and nearly lose my grip on the bench. My legs are so weak that my knees buckle, and Andrei senses this. He promptly scoops me up, turns me back to face him, then lifts me up to straddle him standing up. With my legs wrapped tightly around his waist, he guides his member back to my pulsating hole, penetrating me as he holds me up in his arms. He bounces me up and down on his shaft, slapping my backside and burying his face in my neck to leave more bruising kisses.

Even as my pleasure mounts to a third orgasm, some part of my consciousness is intensely aware of how strong Andrei must be to hold me up like this. I marvel at how well he has kept this animalistic side of him hidden from me until I was ready.

"Ohhh!" I cry out, trembling through my climax.

"*Horoshaya devochka*," he murmurs, his teeth grazing my collarbone.

He starts driving into me faster, his strength unbelievable as he manages to keep me held in his arms even as he begins to lose control completely. He has never used me like this before. The pain gives way to pleasure as I come for the fourth time, and as my hole convulses around him, Andrei bellows out, "*Da, malyshka!*"

With a few quick, hard thrusts, he shoots his seed deep inside me.

We stay there for several minutes just clinging to each other as though we might blow away on the wind if we let go. Andrei covers my face with kisses, making me giggle. We are both drenched with sweat from exertion and from the intense, damp heat of the sauna. I rest my forehead against his and he kisses the tip of my nose. Finally, we get dressed and head back up to the apartment to shower and get ready for bed.

Feeling perfectly loved and protected as I snuggle into bed next to my husband, my heart hardly even aches when my family crosses my mind. I have a new life now. And finally, for the first time, I am truly happy.

ANDREI

*I*'m sitting alone in a bathtub. If my information is good, I don't expect to be hearing noises from the bedroom outside for a few minutes yet. But the curtains are drawn, leaving me shrouded in pale light while I inspect the silenced pistol in my hands.

The bathroom is rather nice, but it isn't as lavish as I'd expect from a man like Kasym Slokavich.

I suppose he's most likely not planning to stay in America long-term. That would explain his heinous behavior over the past few months he's been in New York City. My research on Kasym brought me to places I never thought I'd have to visit again but felt like revisiting old friends — partly because it was, oftentimes.

The lower-ranking Bratva were the only ones who had anything interesting to say about the hedo-

nistic son of Sergei. To the higher ups, he was a
saint, a visionary, and a rising star, particularly
within the sex ring — the industry he's been
partaking in almost nonstop since arriving.

His handlers, the initiates, and the other less
notable muscle tell a very different story. They've
never seen a more violent, abrasive, spoiled, and
lustful human being sweep through the city in all
their short careers put together.

He's been throwing money into the dog fighting
rings for amusement, a business the Bratva usually
leave for the less dignified dregs of the city. Anyone
who dares cross him, he has killed if he doesn't do it
himself.

After I left the auction that fateful night I'd
bought Cassie, Kasym went home with five of the
other girls out of spite that he'd been outbid. Within
a month, all of them turned up dead, a trail of bribes
covering up their disappearances as runaways or
accidents. To hear the pimps talk, his swathe of
bloodshed didn't end there, as Boris's assessment of
the man was true.

To think that Cassie was so close to being bought
by this monster fills me with enough rage to step
outside my profession and murder him with my
own bare hands. I need to kill this man to keep
Cassie safe from him. If he's that bitter about being
outbid, it's only going to be a matter of time before
he goes after what's mine. It is enough to make me

think my dear wife's God does indeed watch out for her.

Even if he must use foul men such as me.

The contract from one of the relatives of the murdered girls calling for Kasym's death could not have been more timely. Nor is it a surprise. I've garnered something of a reputation for such hits since completing the contract that ended Boris's life. I may be the *Shadow*, but witnesses spread rumors, and the woman I saved could not be expected not to talk. I knew it was a liability, but I can no longer turn a blind eye to plights like hers. I have to take action, and I will do so the only way I know how.

And my time making friends in low places has been more of a help than I could ever have imagined. As I gathered information on Kasym, I realized how many of the men are quietly disgruntled with the change in tone he's brought with him to the Bratva. Many of them don't care for his fast and loose life-style, nor for the brutality that inevitably comes with such displays of wealth. He's bringing risk to all our Brotherhood with his brutality, and they all know it's only a matter of time before his carelessness brings us all down. He has no concern with greasing cops, or setting up a fall guy.

More than a few of those connections helped me get here tonight.

I hear the door to the bedroom swing open, muffled through the bathroom door, Kasym's loud laughter roaring and boisterous. There are two other sets of footsteps that accompany his, just as expected.

"...and that dog won me more money than all the other pups that night combined! Ha! To think it was the runt of the litter! Didn't seem so runtish with all that blood on its jaws!" Kasym's voice makes a bizarre barking noise, and the feminine voices with him give a forced laugh at his disgusting antics.

"Now you," he says to one of them, "get to start with me early. You," he says presumably to the other, "go get yourself cleaned up before the fun. Don't want you stinking up the new sheets."

"I won't keep you waiting too long," the voice of the second woman teases, but I can hear the fear behind her voice.

The bathroom door opens, and I remain deathly still. She knows I'm behind the curtain, but whether she can pretend she doesn't may jeopardize the entire hit. She closes the door and runs the water in the sink, and the moment she thinks she's out of earshot of Kasym, I hear her suppress a sob. I want desperately to tap the side of the tub to remind her this is all part of the game, but I know I have to resist.

I hear her freshen up a bit before stripping some of the clothes from her body and stepping back outside.

"All yours, baby," she says, and she's soon

answered by a dark chuckle from Kasym. I can already hear the first woman grinding on him, her breathy gasps loud and forced — that much is obvious to someone who's heard the real thing.

I wait only a minute. I hear Kasym's voice whispering to the girls as they begin their work on him, and I know we have a time limit to work with.

Stealthy as a wolf, I rise from my position in the bath and very slowly pull the curtain back.

The sex worker who had been in the bathroom had left the door open but nearly shut, and something on the mirror caught my eye. She'd used the lipstick she was applying to write a message on the corner of the mirror:

*First moan*

I cock my gun and put my shoulder against the door gingerly, waiting, listening. Contact like this is dangerous, because there's so much room for error or miscommunication. Every small gasp I hear faked from the girls in the room could make me twitch, but I wait, a bead of sweat rolling down my forehead as I prepare for the most dangerous hit of my life.

Then, an unmistakable cry of feigned ecstasy.

I shove the door open, and as I do, like clockwork, the two naked women on either side of Kasym in his satin-sheeted bed seize one of his arms and pin him down. Kasym, his eyes wide as baseballs and his body naked and exposed, hardly has time to react before I step forward, my face stony as a statue of a saint, and I unload three rounds into him: two to the chest, then one to the head.

In all of two seconds, it's over.

The women had held their heads down the moment I pushed the door open, bracing for what would happen. It was such a risk, having them so close like that, but it was one they had volunteered for when I contacted them for information about the hit.

Sex workers all over the state knew and hated Kasym. He was hurting them, and no doubt word has spread not to take him as a client, leaving him to prey on only the most vulnerable girls.

And now they were free from him forever.

The two women leap out of the bed and back away from the pool of blood soaking into the sheets around the man, but neither of them look away.

"Thank fuck," one of them murmurs.

"What now?" asks the other.

"Now," I say as I step forward to inspect the body, "the two of you need to disappear. Things are going to get very hot, very soon."

"The goons outside won't give you any trouble?" the second asks.

"No. They're almost as tired of these rich bastards' abuses as you are. The staff tonight is who got me here in the first place."

The two of them exchange glances, then nod. "We'll get the word around that this fucker's dead.

Make it sound like someone on the inside did him in, maybe put the fear of God back in the higher-ups."

I give a single nod. "Good."

"You gonna be okay?"

I glance at her briefly. "Don't worry about me. I was never here."

The door opens, and one of the bodyguards with an uzi at his side peers in. We exchange a look, and he nods, beckoning me out to the escape route he has planned.

Despite all my precaution, I know this is almost a foolishly brazen move on my part, but I had to do it to keep Cassie safe. I may have succeeded in rallying the blue-collar criminals against the sex ring in New York, but silence can't be assured from so many people, even in the best of conditions.

There may be retaliation from this. The only question is how much the Bratva still knows about me.

CASSIE

*I* wake up from a pleasant dream just past midnight to a horrifying, loud crack followed by the sounds of glass shattering. I sit up ramrod straight in bed, looking around in terror. For a moment, some part of my brain tries to dismiss the sounds as psychosomatic, just figments of my hazy, sleepy mind. But then the bedroom door bursts open and Andrei comes bolting in. Blinking my eyes in the low light, I can just make out his grim expression and panicked eyes. I have never seen him look like this. Andrei is never afraid. Never.

As he rushes to my side I grab for him and ask, "What was that? What happened? I heard a horrible noise — "

"Nothing, *printsessa*, but I need you to get up and put on some warm clothes for me, okay? It's time for us to go," Andrei says, helping me out of bed and running to grab me a sweater and a coat. As I ease into the sleeves of the sweater, struggling to pull it closed over my bulging stomach in my nightdress and warm leggings, I look up at him in confusion. The clock reads 12:17. Where would we possibly have to go in the middle of the night? What is going on?

"Where are we going?"

Andrei yanks a duffel bag out of the closet and starts stuffing random sweaters and pants into it — all winter clothing, though it isn't even that cool outside anymore. He doesn't answer me as he hurriedly tosses a pair of boots my way and squishes several thick scarves into the bag.

"Andrei!" I cry, stomping my foot. "What are we doing?"

"Put on the boots," he says simply, not even looking up.

Crossing my arms over my chest, I fight the urge to just give in and submit to his order, standing my ground. This is insane!

"Not until you tell me what's going on."

Finally he looks over at me, fixing me with one of those cold, hard glares. A chill runs down my spine. I know he is angry — even if the anger isn't actually directed at me.

"Cassie. Please. We need to leave, now."

His voice is low and deliberate, and I sigh, sitting down to pull on the boots. Andrei opens a box in the back of the closet, one I have never noticed before, and withdraws a little blue booklet, along with a manila folder filled with some official-looking documents. He stuffs these items into the front zipper pocket of the duffel bag, as well as a thick wad of hundred dollar bills.

"What is all that for?" I demand to know, running up to him and trying to unzip the bag.

Andrei catches me in his arms and holds me by the shoulders, peering into my eyes.

"You have to trust me, *lapochka*. It is my job to keep you safe, and I will do exactly that. But you have to listen to me and do as I say," he explains softly. Suddenly I am truly afraid. Keep me safe? From what?

"Okay," I reply weakly.

Andrei grabs the duffel bag, takes me by the hand, and leads me quickly out of the bedroom into the living room. There is a loud zinging noise as something impossibly small and fast whizzes by just in front of us, putting a hole in the wall. I scream and fall back into Andrei's arms, my heart racing.

"Wh-what was that?" I ask, my eyes huge.

Andrei holds me close and covers me with his body as we rush out of the apartment, down the hall, and into the elevator. I'm still shaking when we reach the ground floor lobby, Andrei nearly carrying me as we run out to his Corvette in the parking garage.

ALEXIS ABBOTT

"Andrei!" I shout, tears in my eyes. "I'm scared! Please tell me what is happening!"

"There's no time," he says flatly, easing me into the back seat and throwing the duffel bag in the trunk. I put my hands protectively over my pregnant belly, looking out the windows.

"Why can't I sit up there with you?" I ask, leaning over the console as Andrei slides into the driver's seat and starts the engine. We peel out of the parking garage just as another car zooms out of a spot just a few rows away and quickly falls in behind us.

"Get down!" Andrei shouts, spinning the wheel so that the car turns a sharp corner, slinging me back into the seat. "Lay down on the seat! Don't sit up for anything, don't look out the windows!"

I fall back on my side, curling my legs up to my belly and wrapping my arms around the unborn child inside me, whispering nonsensical words of comfort to him as though he could hear me. We fly around corners so fast that I feel the tires come up off the road slightly, the Corvette drifting around hairpin turns. It occurs to me that Andrei is trying to shake off someone who is tailing us.

Somebody is chasing us.

Probably the same people who fired into our living room.

"What are we gonna do?" I whimper, tears rolling down my cheeks.

"You're going someplace safe, *moya lyubova*. Don't you worry."

"Who's after us?"

"Bad people. You don't need to think about that. Just focus on yourself and that little baby, okay? I promise everything will work out, just trust me."

Finally, the wild, sudden turns give way to an engine-roaring, pedal-to-the-floor increase in speed as we shoot straight forward down what I assume is a highway. I know we've got to be driving at least thirty over the speed limit, but Andrei doesn't slow the car at all.

"Did we lose them?" I ask, sounding very frail and terrified.

"For now, yes. But we have to hurry," Andrei answers. Then, in a more serious tone, he continues. "Listen to me, *malyshka*. I am going to take care of everything. You're going ahead of me, and I know you'll be scared, but just know that I will be right behind you. Everything is already set up and you have nothing to worry about. They already know you're coming —"

"They? Who? Where?" I ask, sitting up in the seat against Andrei's orders.

I see that we are pulling down a dirt road, barreling along the narrow path through the thick trees, branches scraping the sides of the Corvette. Andrei doesn't seem to care; he is completely focused on the road ahead. Finally the car screeches to a stop in front of a small building with a massive black concrete field behind it. Peeking through the trees is what looks to be... a small airplane.

"No," I murmur under my breath. Andrei leaps out of the car, takes the duffel bag out of the trunk, and starts wheeling it away, beckoning for me to follow.

I reluctantly get out of the car and hurry after him, holding my belly.

"*Mi prishli*, Pavel!" he calls out as we run to the little concrete structure. A short, squat, bespectacled man with receding brown hair and a bearded face full of laugh lines peeks out of the door, gesturing for us to hurry inside.

"*Toropis!*" the man barks at us. "Come on!"

He ushers us in, takes the duffel bag, and starts waddling away toward the plane outside. But then suddenly he turns around and does a double-take, blinking rapidly as he looks me up and down. He adjusts his tiny, round-frame glasses and then frowns at me, shaking his head. He folds his arms over his chest and gives Andrei a dubious look.

"What is it? We have to hurry!" Andrei hisses at him, his large frame towering over Pavel's in an almost comical way.

But the older man clucks his tongue. "*Gospodin Petrov*, you know I cannot fly her."

Andrei rounds on him, aggressively reaching for the man's collar, but Pavel moves out of the way and points accusingly at me — more specifically, at my pregnant belly.

"*Slishkom opasno*! She is too *beremenna*! Bad for the baby!" Pavel exclaims.

Andrei's face hardens and he looks at me with panic in his eyes.

"Are you sure? Is there really no way?" he asks.

The smaller man shakes his head. "Not safe, *moy drug*. I cannot take her in good conscience. The flight to *Sibir* is long and hard."

"*Sibir*?" I repeat, the word falling from my mouth awkwardly. Then it dawns on me. "Siberia? You're sending me to Yakutsk?" I shout, backing away and holding my arms over my stomach instinctively.

Andrei hurries forward to take me in his arms, even though I fight him in vain. He pulls me close and kisses the top of my head, soothing me with his stroking hands.

"You would have been safe there to wait for my return, Cassie," he assures me. Then, looking over at Pavel, he asks, "Is there no other choice? Is there nowhere else?"

Pavel sighs and puts his hands on his hips, tapping his foot thoughtfully. "Well, I might have someplace you could go, for now. *Moya sestra*... she has a commercial property just north of here off the interstate. A warehouse. *Pustoy*. Funding fell through and now it's just sitting there, unused." He gives some directions in Russian I can't even begin to follow.

Andrei is already nodding and leading me out of the building to the car. He calls over his shoulder, "And you will tell her we're coming?"

"*Da, da.* Of course," Pavel calls in response, waving his hand dismissively.

We get back into the car and speed away down the dirt road back to the highway, crossing quickly onto the interstate. It only takes us half an hour to reach our destination, and it is a pure miracle that we aren't pulled over for speeding on the way.

Finally breaking my silence as he pulls me out of the car and guides me toward the big, looming gray warehouse, I spit, "You were going to just send me away like my parents did?"

Andrei looks at me with genuine hurt in his eyes, and I immediately regret my accusatory tone. Shifting the duffel bag on his shoulder as he opens a weather-beaten side door, he answers quietly, "No, Cassie. I would never do that to you. I would have followed you there once it was safe to do so."

"Safe from what?" I press him.

He closes the door behind us and flicks a light on. After a second of flickering hesitation, a fluorescent light hums to light far overhead. It's still quite dim, but at least now we can see where we're going. The huge building is musty and eerie, completely abandoned yet clean enough to indicate that someone still intends to make something of it. There are big boxes stacked in ten-foot piles, and Andrei leads me toward what looks to be a tiny, nondescript office.

Once inside the office room, he sits me down on a dusty swivel chair and finally answers my question. "Cassie, *moya printsessa*, there are bad people who want to hurt me… and you."

"Who are they?" I ask, my heart pounding.

"I'm sure you have guessed by now that I do not have a, ahh, traditional job."

I cock my head to the side and look at him critically. "I know that sometimes you leave in the night and come back in the morning looking… different."

Andrei stares down at the ugly brown carpet. "Yes."

"I always worried that it might be something dangerous."

"Yes."

I pause, searching his face for answers. I am scared to ask anything else, scared to shatter the quickly-dilapidating illusion of our stability, our happy life together.

"Andrei, just tell me. What is going on?"

Finally, he looks up and meets my eyes. He looks impossibly sad.

"*Ubiytsa*. That is the word for what I am." The word is heavy, but I don't understand it.

"But what does that mean?" I press, my hands absently rubbing my belly.

"It means that for many years I have killed men for money," Andrei answers simply.

My heart stops for a split second and I feel myself go cold, my head turning fuzzy, as though I might faint. Surely he doesn't mean that. It's ridiculous. My Andrei, my Prince Charming, my doting husband — he cannot be a cold-blooded murderer.

"No... that's not true. It can't be," I say, my voice scarcely above a whisper.

Andrei nods slowly. "Yes, Cassie. It is true. I am sorry for keeping it from you, but I did not want to involve you, and I did not want you to fear me."

"Fear you?" I repeat, starting to cry. "I... I am starting to wonder if I even *know* you."

He looks paralyzed with remorse, with hurt. But I cannot take back what I've said.

"No, no, *malyshka*, you know me. The real me. I swear to you I have never shown anyone the side of me that you have seen. And you have changed me for the better," he says quickly, moving forward to kneel in front of me, reaching for my hands.

I snatch them away and he looks heartbroken.

"How can I trust you, knowing that you have committed the most terrible sins?" I ask him honestly. "You are the father of my child, this little innocent inside me. But you... you hurt people for a living? *Kill* them?"

"Only the bad ones, I swear. And I have found my calling, Cassie. I have vowed to protect those who

are good, who are victims, and those who are innocent. Like our son."

I look at him hard, weighing his words against
the screaming voice in my head telling me to
condemn him, to turn away and never look back.

But I can't do that. Because I love him. And
because he is right: I do know him. I know the real
Andrei Petrov, the man who rescued me from that
awful basement and made me happier than I've ever
been. I never told him but I'd heard the things the
people in that crowd were saying to me, and now I
have the understanding to know what they meant.
They wanted to assault me, to hurt me. They
laughed about it. But Andrei has never even raised
his voice to me, even though I've been abandoned by
everyone else I know and love. There's no one to
protect me from him, but I've never needed protection from him.

He is the man I have been waiting for, even
though I never knew it. And I must accept him, no
matter what, as he has accepted me.

"I swear to you, Cassie, I only do this now to rid
the world of evil. I want to make the world a safer
place for our child to grow up in. I want to shield
you from pain and danger, and I will never stop
protecting you, no matter what. Please let me prove
myself to you."

"You don't have to," I reply. "I know exactly what
you are."

There is a long pause before I take a deep breath and continue.

"You are my husband. And I will follow you anywhere. I took a vow, Andrei, and I will not turn my back on that promise. I love you more than you can ever know, and I will stay with you through thick and thin. But you must swear to me one thing."

Andrei takes my hands in his and kisses them. "Anything."

"Don't send me away," I say, my voice cracking as tears spring to my eyes.

My husband stands up and takes me in his arms, cradling me to his chest.

"Of course, *moya lyubova*," he assures me, kissing the top of my head. "Never again."

# ANDREI

"So, Kasym, h-he's really dead, then?"

"Yes," I answer, taking a sip of coffee as I stare intensely at the man whose life I'd spared just a few nights before meeting Cassie, "and now it's time for me to call in the favor, Mr. Jackson. A life for a life."

Jackson runs his hand through his hair, striding around the room of the safe house he's been living in since I put him there all those months ago. And soon, he won't have to live here ever again.

"And you're sure Kasym is the one who...who..." Jackson swallows, wringing his hands. Even in hiding, he's only become a more nervous man than he was before.

"Who ordered the hit on you, yes," I answer calmly, "he acted through an agent to hire me. I only found out more when I was digging up dirt on the man himself before carrying out the act. All I found out about you was that you were an innocent cab driver. Now, I need you to think very carefully. Why did Kasym want you dead, Jackson?"

I've been bringing food and water to Mr. Jackson at this unassuming safe house far upstate, far from anywhere the Bratva would care to stick their noses, ever since I faked his assassination. He was an innocent man, certainly not deserving of the death my client at the time had asked for him. Most of my targets had been dregs who deserved such punishment, in one way or another, but Jackson...he was totally benign. Just a bystander someone wanted slain.

And now I see why. Kasym's arbitrary cruelty knew no bounds.

Jackson wrings his hands and sits on the couch, biting his lip as he speaks. "I...I think...the only thing I can think of seems too absurd-"

"Nothing is out of reason for someone like Kasym." I'm trying to prove a specific piece of information with Jackson's account. I'm almost sure of the answer, but I need to hear this from a witness before I act on something this big.

"Well," he hesitates, "the only time I met him was when I drove him from the airport to the apartment complex he was going to. He was completely trashed when he got off that plane, I mean absolutely blitzed. His bodyguard had to practically carry him."

I nod, taking a few paces around the room as I drink my coffee and he speaks.

"H-he kept rambling drunkenly on the way, like he was bragging. His English was broken, but he kept talking about how he was going to 'rule this town' because of his dad."

Now I *know* I'm onto something, and I watch Jackson intently.

"He went on and on about how rich they were, and he said his dad was bringing him home so he could take over as the next 'king of the whores' and that he was going to spend all his time here enjoying his 'dad's empire.' "

My face goes pale as I hear the piece of information I need to hear. It all makes sense now.

"So," I say slowly, "Sergei Slokavich isn't as much of a buffoon as he lets on — he's the kingpin of the local sex trafficking ring."

"Oh my god," Jackson says, his head sinking into his hands, "I drove around the son of a crime lord?!"

"And he wanted you dead after he realized how much he'd said when he sobered up," I explain before finishing my coffee and setting the cup down. "You're very lucky to be alive, Mr. Jackson."

"But for how long?!" he splutters, and I hold up a hand to silence him.

"Patience, Mr. Jackson. You've been a very great help to me here. I know what needs to be done now. I will contact you as soon as it's done, but know that you're going to help a great many people by your actions."

Jackson looks at me for a long time, then nods slowly, sitting back on the couch and resting his head on the back of it. "That's all I know. I swear."

"Rest easy, Mr. Jackson," I say, heading towards the door and starting on the dozen or so deadbolts, "your would-be killer is on your side, and the man who gave the order is dead — and what's more, I'm about to pay the true mastermind a long overdue visit."

*But first,* I think privately, *there's someone far more precious I must see to before putting myself in an incredibly dangerous position.*

CASSIE

*I*n the three days I've spent in the safehouse, I have been surprisingly okay. Despite the looming fear of being found and the constant surroundings of an abandoned warehouse, Andrei has managed to keep me from going totally mad. He's only left my side once, and not for very long. I did not ask him what he did when he left. It's easier this way.

It turns out that he has always had some form of a back-up plan like this stored away for quick use, and therefore we are shockingly prepared for this kind of situation. From his Corvette, which he keeps under a black tarp outside, he retrieves a laptop with a built-in Internet access device, bedrolls, blankets, bottled water, non-perishable snacks, and a rudimentary hygiene kit. To his surprise and my infinite relief, we discover that the safehouse has a utilitarian shower stall in the bathroom. Thanks to the fact that Pavel's sister stubbornly refused to let this building fall completely into disrepair and uselessness, the water still runs. It's icy cold water, but it's certainly preferable to going indefinitely without washing.

We have wiled away the time by watching soap operas (which I have grown very attached to) on his laptop, cuddling, and experimenting with trying to make palatable meals out of the basic foods Andrei's kept stashed in his emergency rations. I have been increasingly hungry as time goes on, with the little life inside me getting bigger and bigger by the day. Sometimes my body hurts so badly that I want to cry, but Andrei comforts me, tending to my every ache and complaint like a trained nurse.

In the long, dull hours since we first showed up here, we have talked more and had deeper conversations than we have in the time we've been married collectively. He tells me about his difficult childhood growing up in the world's coldest city, and I tell him about my own repressed youth.

Lying on our bedrolls, which we have lined up beside each other to make a sort of makeshift double bed, Andrei asks, "You never went to school like other children?"

"No," I reply, shaking my head. "My parents... they insisted that public schools were dens of temptation and sinful thought. My father used to say that the Board of Education was staffed entirely by soldiers of Satan."

Andrei laughs, a sound which I've heard more of in the past three days than I ever have before, despite the grimness of our situation. "I don't know how public schooling is here in America, but back home it was one of the few places where I could feel safe. And warm."

"I don't know how you survived it," I murmur, in awe of his tenacity.

"The streets of Yakutsk are not a suitable home for a young boy, it is true. But at least I did find a few people who were helpful. Sonya's mother, the owner of the fish market, made sure that I ate on the coldest winter nights when I could not afford food. I feel guilty for stealing from her market, but she always knew that I did it. She watched me from a distance, and did not stop me when I stole fish or rabbits from her stands."

"I hope that someday she will get to see Sonya again," I muse aloud. "I know she must miss her daughter terribly. And Sonya is so wonderful."

"*Da*," Andrei agrees. "She takes after her mother in that way."

After a pause, I say slowly, "I wonder if I will ever see my family again. Well, mostly I just miss Isaiah."

"Your *dorogoy bratik*," he says, nodding. "Well, perhaps someday."

"But I wouldn't even know how to keep *us* safe,

much less protect him from whoever is after us," I lament, fidgeting with the blankets. Andrei suddenly sits up.

"That reminds me," he begins, getting to his feet.

"Where are you going?"

"The car. I will be back. Stay there."

I lay back on the bedroll, rubbing my stomach, feeling around for the familiar kick of my unborn son. "How are you doing, little one?" I coo. "Everything is going to be alright, I promise. I love you more than you will ever understand."

Just then, there's the surreal, beautiful sensation I've been waiting for. A kick.

When Andrei comes back from the car, I call out to him excitedly, "Come feel the baby! He's kicking, Andrei! He heard me talking to him!"

He rushes into the office and kneels down beside me, setting one hand down on my stomach, looking at me with expectant, joyous eyes. There it is. Another tiny, barely perceptible kick from the tiny child I'm carrying.

Andrei's face lights up and he kisses my protruding belly sweetly. It's then that I notice the gun in his hand. I gasp and point to it fearfully.

"What is that? Get it away from us!" I exclaim, trying and failing to wriggle away.

He hurriedly shakes his head and takes my hand. "No, *malyshka*, it's okay. I promise. The safety is on. You're not in any danger."

"I don't like guns," I tell him firmly, eyeing the black device.

"I know. I don't expect you to. But there may come a time when you will have to use one," Andrei explains carefully. "I will do everything in my power to protect you, and that also means that I must give you a way to protect yourself."

After a long minute of silent tension, I relent.

"Only for the sake of the baby," I tell him.

*"Khoroshaya devochka,"* Andrei says, gently placing the gun in my hand. "I will teach you how to use it. I pray that you will never have to, but I need you to be prepared."

"I understand," I answer dutifully.

*T*he small wooden confinements around me creak ominously, and I find myself doing something I'd never think I'd be doing so intensely before — relying on the skills of others.

I'm being carried in a sealed wooden container by several of Sergei Slokavich's henchmen. They're the only ones who could get me onto the grounds of his estate without my being riddled with bullets within a matter of seconds. There is no client for this job. In the aftermath of slaying his beloved son, I need to deal with Sergei as a personal matter.

Indeed, my move against Sergei by killing his son caused some waves. It gave the lower ranks of the Bratva the inspiration they needed to take action against the old and increasingly corrupt regime. There have already been rumors of smuggling rings going rogue, distributing their profit amongst one another instead of their bosses. And some of the enforcers even drove out the dogfighting rings Kasym had brought in.

But I suppose I have Kasym and Kasym alone to thank for my ability to be smuggled into the manor tonight, so I should be more grateful.

I'm hiding inside his coffin.

It's being transported to the manor prior to the body's move from the morgue. Sergei wants to make sure everything is perfect for the small, quiet ceremony he and his circle of confidantes will hold. Mobsters like Sergei and his kind rarely hold funerals as public affairs. It's too dangerous, they've decided, after having several such funerals shot up by rivals.

It's a long ride inside my confinements, and I'm totally blind — betrayal at this stage would be the easiest thing in the world, and Sergei would no doubt reward my pallbearers generously for handing me over to him.

It's a tense wait. While I'm used to taking calculated risks like this, now I have a woman and a child to care for. To protect. And if this ends with me being pumped full of bullets from an automatic already in the coffin, they will suffer. That weighs on me like nothing ever has before in a mission.

But after what seems like an eternity, I feel myself being lowered down, and footsteps shuffle away quickly. I wait another five minutes before pushing the top off quietly, having made sure the hinges were well-oiled before undertaking this ludicrous mission. When I stand up, I find myself in a cool and dry basement, surrounded by nothing but a few other crates and miscellany.

The common muscle truly does want the regime deposed badly enough to work and sacrifice together.

I slip up the stairs quietly, checking each step before putting my full weight on it. A few of the recently hired men who got me in might be on my side, but the staff within these manor walls are unlikely to be so accommodating. At least, not on short notice.

Starting to stick my head out the door to the hallway, I pull back inside as an armed patrol passes by. He's clad in a gray jacket that his hand is hidden inside, and I don't have to guess what he's packing in there.

This isn't the kind of security one expects on an average day, even for a crime lord. Sergei is expecting me.

I reach into my jacket and pull out the hard little black object I brought along for the job tonight. I check the opposite direction down the hallway before slipping up after the guard silently and bringing the blackjack down over his head. In an instant, he's out cold.

I catch him as he falls and lift him up over my

shoulder, making sure to remove the pistol falling from his hand and stow it in my belt. I know I can't be far from a storage room at this level of the estate.

It isn't difficult to find one, and I quickly carry my man inside and close the door behind me. The room seems to be used for food storage, as there are crates of dry goods and fresh produce laid out on tables, presumably for the reception of Kasym's funeral.

I set the guard onto the ground and strip him in a matter of seconds. In less than a minute, I've donned his coat and trousers, and I'm able to pull the collar of the jacket up to obscure my face. To the staff, I won't be distinguishable from any of the other guards newly brought inside for this job.

After binding and gagging the guard with a spare tablecloth, I store him inside a pantry and head back out.

As soon as I'm in the hallway again, my heart skips a beat as I see a maid a few yards ahead of me. She turns to glance at me as I come out...and to my relief, she turns back and carries on her way.

I make haste in the opposite direction.

I make my way swiftly up several flights of stairs, moving as quietly as possible. I've had the good fortune of having been to this manor before.

And a hitman never forgets the layout of a building.

The smell of fine wood and rich, expensive

carpeting accompanies me as I move up the stairs. It's a strange contrast for the Sergei I know, the sleazy, skeevy Bratva boss on his way to some other hedonistic diversion. But the relatively pristine state of the house is telling that he spends very little time here; the place hardly seems lived-in.

But I know my information is good. He's here, and he's scared.

He has a study-office on the top floor. I make my way to the floor just below that, then take a left into the long hallway. The security on the top floor will be even tighter right now, if I know Sergei.

So I make my way down the hall towards a bedroom I stayed in the one time I visited this place. I was here on business, one of the first times I met Sergei. A mutual friend was introducing us, and I remember loathing the man from the very start.

But even with that gut instinct, I never thought I'd be where I am today.

I push open the door to the old guest room, and the door bumps into the butler who was half a pace to the door handle.

He looks apologetic for a moment, until he gets a good look at my face.

"Wait, you're not —"

I'm on him in an instant, one of my hands wrapping around his head, covering his mouth, the other hand pointing the gun at his head.

"I'm not going to kill you," I whisper as the man

trembles in my grasp, his eyes focusing on the gun barrel. "I'm going to end this. But I need information."

I feel his head give an almost imperceptible nod, the man clearly too afraid to make any sudden movements.

"That window there," I nod my head towards the open curtains at the far end of the room, near the bed, "will the guards be looking up at them? Monitoring the windows, the roof?"

There's a pause as the butler thinks, then he gives his head a quick shake, looking up at me in no small measure of terror — but honesty.

"Good. I'm about to release you. Go into that closet by the door and hide. You'll know when it's time to leave."

I let the man go, and he takes a breath, grasping his throat for a moment before scurrying off to obey my orders without a moment wasted. I make my way towards the window.

Sliding it open, the night air greets me, but I only savor it for a breath before climbing up on the railing and crawling up the side of the brick wall.

I glance at the grounds below as I go. The gardens are crawling with guards — it would have been impossible to get here without my allies on the inside.

Gliding along the wall like a shadow, keeping far out of the lights from below, I move past the top floor and leap onto the slanted rooftop, crouching low as I make my way to the opposite side of the house.

The butler was wrong, I realize as a noise pricks my ears. There was at least one guard up here. I press myself up against a chimney in the darkness and wait for him to walk by before slipping up behind the man and dispatching him with the black-jack as I had the first.

Without any more time to waste, I move to the opposite edge of the rooftop.

A small trail of smoke is spiralling up from the balcony below. I know who it belongs to.

As I crane my neck over the side, I see Sergei Slokavich, leaning on the balcony railing and surveying the grounds below with a cigar in his hand. He's wearing only a silk bathrobe. When I speak, I address him in Russian.

"Even if you scream, the guards won't be here in time."

As Sergei whirls around with the pistol he was hiding in his robe, I'm already halfway down upon him, snatching the weapon as if it were a toy and turning it on him an instant after landing.

He holds his hands up, his face pale as he sees me standing over him, his own revolver pointed at his skull. Nevertheless, there's something troublingly calm in his eyes as he watches me, and after a moment, he even begins to smile.

"So," he answers in our mother language, "the attack dog turns on its master."

"You still think I ever cared to be a slave to the likes of you?"

"I know you do. It's in your blood. I'm your family, Andrei," he hisses, "the Bratva brought you in, raised you, made you what you are! You owe us everything, and this is how you repay us?"

My mind flashes to the faces of Cassie's parents, coldly giving her away to be sold off like a piece of meat at the market. "Sometimes, family ties have their limits. You've gone too far, Sergei. The common soldiers of the Bratva know that."

"Bullshit," he snarls back, sneering. "You are just like the rest of them. You know what all of you are? A bunch of minnows swimming in a sea of big fish." He pounds his chest, narrowing his eyes at me. "Sharks like me? Sometimes we let you little fish swim alongside us. We give you food from the kills we make, we give you protection from the other sharks that would have you for lunch if you were left alone, and we even go out of our way to give you a little fun on the side. You, Andrei? You're just my shadow. The shadow of a shark that some of the other little fish want to flock to."

Now it's my turn to smile.

"Had time to think that one out, did you? Is that what you tell yourself when you're selling off women's lives as if they were cattle? Letting people get slaughtered for your pet project your son was? Something you should have remembered, Sergei," I say as I cock my gun, "if you treat people like animals, don't be surprised when they hunt you down like one."

He lets out a cruel laugh into the night. "Heroic, but too late, my shadow." I arch a brow, and he nods to the cell phone sitting on the balcony railing. "You don't think I knew you were coming for me? Didn't think I'd find your little safehouse?"

My heart stands still a moment as Sergei's eyes narrow at me, his grin showing off his rotting, stained teeth. "I gave the order before you even jumped down here. Your little bride is already dead."

With a roar, I lurch forward and seize Sergei Slokavich by the neck, hurling him over the side of the railing and off the balcony, watching his face contort into a scream as he falls down four stories, and there's a sickening sound as he lands on the tip of the fountain below, the stone point sticking out of his impaled body. His lifeless eyes stare up at me as a handful of alarmed guards gather around him, looking up at the balcony and pointing.

But I'm already gone, flying through the house like a spectre.

A shadow cannot exist without its light.

## CASSIE

*I*'m sitting in the office of the warehouse in the dark, the room lit only by the unnatural glow of a laptop screen. The little digital clock in the corner of the screen reads 2:27 AM. My nails, formerly smooth and painted bright pink at one of the many salons Andrei took me to, have been bitten down to the quick. I'm shivering, even though I'm perched under three blankets, my legs folded under me on the bedroll. At this point in my pregnancy, this is the closest to comfortable I can possibly manage. Standing up for too long is agony. I've tried lying down on my back, my left side, my right side — nothing works. So I just sit.

If I'd been spending all this time alone, I surely would have lost my mind by now. The cold silence and dull, tedious surroundings make a powerful case for cabin fever — a term I learned from a series of excessive, boredom-induced Wikipedia searches. But with Andrei around, the time has been significantly less awful. He's been so sweet and attentive, even talkative. But now he's left me here. I'm not sure where he's gone to, but I know exactly what he is going there to do.

He's going to kill the man who's forced us to hide here.

Underneath the pile of blankets, my left hand rests on my stomach, gently rubbing slow circles over the protruding bump there. These motions are just as much to soothe myself as they are meant to comfort the baby inside. He kicks every now and then, as if to remind me that he's here with me still. And my right hand... well, it's wrapped around the handle of a gun.

The safety is off and I dare not even approach the trigger for fear of accidentally firing the shiny little widow-maker. I wonder to myself if my unborn son can sense how frightened I am, how close he is in proximity to a powerful weapon. I hope with all my racing heart that he can't tell where we are or what's going on. I would never wish this kind of terror on anyone, much less my own tiny child. The laptop screen goes dark as it's sat untouched for too long, leaving me totally blind. A shiver runs a cold trail down my spine.

"It's okay, little one," I murmur, my voice thin and shaking. "Daddy will be back soon, I'm sure.

He's going to make everything alright and we'll get to leave this place for good. And as soon as he gets back I'm going to throw this stupid gun into a dumpster. Or a volcano."

At first when Andrei showed me — carefully — how to use it, I told him over and over that I would sooner die than fire a gun. But then he reminded me that I'm not just carrying it to protect myself — it's our son's life I must protect, as well. He told me that once this is over, I will never have to so much as look at a gun again for the rest of my life. He promised me that this would be the end of the terror, the end of the war.

For that's what it feels like right now. I am a fugitive, hiding in the dark. The forces of evil are stalking me, desperately trying to pin down my location so they can finally put an end to me and my baby. But I refuse to give in so easily. The old Cassandra would be cowering, completely inconsolable, totally hysterical with panic.

But right now I am surprisingly calm. Sure, my hands are shaking and my stomach is twisting in knots, but I'm done hiding. My strong, noble husband is out there somewhere, finding the big boss so he can chop off the head of the snake and put an end to this. He's on the offense.

It is my job to maintain the defense here.

I know I'm in danger. Andrei has already explained to me that these men are totally ruthless, that they'll do anything in their power to stop him — to *hurt* him. And he says that they know about me now. They know how to hit him where it really hurts: his heart.

That means me. And our son.

So I've got to be strong, for the three of us. I clench my teeth, staring into the darkness expectantly. I don't know what is going to come through that door first: my husband, returning triumphantly from battle, or some lowlife criminal, hell-bent on using me and my baby as bargaining chips. Or as collateral. Or… just to kill us for the sake of killing.

I shudder to myself but won't look away from the direction of the door. I must stay vigilant and patient while the war rages far beyond these walls.

"I swear I'm going to give you the happiest life any little boy could have," I whisper, patting my stomach. "You're going to have a toy boat, and a teddy bear, and a —"

Just then, a small sliver of light pierces the darkness.

The door is slowly, slowly opening. I hold my breath, too afraid to even blink. Under my left hand, my baby kicks. I pray silently, desperately, that it's because his father is approaching. It must be Andrei. It has to be.

Still, I tighten my grip on the gun.

The shaft of light across the floor widens ever so slightly as somebody walks into the warehouse. I strain my eyes and ears, watching and listening for any hint, any trace of my husband. I listen closely to the approaching footsteps, hoping to somehow discern from their weight and rhythm whether they belong to Andrei. But it's a futile attempt. In my current state of paralyzed terror combined with the pitch-black darkness, I have no idea who is walking in.

The footfalls are heavy, dragging. They don't sound like my husband, who is surprisingly light-footed in spite of his size. But I could be wrong. What if it *is* Andrei, and he's hurt? A limp of some kind would certainly account for the change in gait. My heart pounds so loudly that I worry the intruder might hear it and be able to find me that way.

The column of light suddenly dissipates, leaving the three of us in total darkness: me, my unborn son, and the mysterious, possibly lethal stranger walking slowly toward us.

My head grows fuzzy as it dawns on me that I've been holding my breath this whole time. My lungs are so tightly constricted in my chest that my body aches, from more than just pregnancy pain. I have to take a breath before I pass out.

So I do. One quick, sharp inhale.

And that's all it takes.

There's a deafening crack — the unmistakable sound of a gun firing at mid-range. In the split second following, I gasp and close my eyes tightly, wrapping my left arm around my stomach, my mind going totally blank with fear as I brace myself for the inevitable pain.

But it doesn't come. Instead, the office window breaks with a hail of broken glass and the laptop to my right shatters in a spark of electrical light, plastic bits flying. I scream involuntarily, and in response I hear a deep, cruel laugh.

He yells something in Russian that I don't understand.

"Leave us alone!" I cry, fumbling to get a solid grip on the gun. Everything is still totally dark — I can't even tell what direction the voice is coming from, other than vaguely in front of me. Trembling, gritting my teeth so hard it makes my jaw ache, I lift up the gun and point it weakly before me.

"*Vremya umirat!*" he snarls.

I hear the distinct, horrifying sound of a gun cocking.

Before I have even a nanosecond to think about it, I pull the trigger.

The gun pops with such a powerful, loud jolt that it falls from my hand. There's a strangled shout and then the sound of something heavy collapsing to the floor. I hyperventilate, rocking back and forth with both arms wrapped protectively around my belly. I have no idea if I have killed my attacker or if he is simply wounded and preparing to shoot at me again

— but I know that I simply cannot bring myself to fire the gun another time.

Just then, the warehouse door swings open with a bang, admitting a wide column of moonlight to break through the shadows, the silhouette of a tall, broad-shouldered man in the doorway. Several yards in front of him, the dim light just barely illuminates the still, lifeless body of the intruder.

"Andrei?" I call out, my voice wavering. I am too frightened to even consider the possibility that this second person might be yet another enemy.

"Cassie!"

It's Andrei's voice. My heartbeat quickens and tears burn in my eyes as I struggle to get to my feet. I need to be near him, now. I need to hold him in my arms and make absolutely certain that he is real, that he's alive.

He bolts toward me, sidestepping the dead body in front of him, bursting through the office door and sweeping me into his arms. He smells like gunpowder, like death — and yet, when he kisses the top of my head, I feel more alive than ever.

"*Moya lyubova*, are you alright? Oh, my sweet *zhena*!" he murmurs, covering my face with kisses, his hands gripping me like he is afraid I'll dematerialize at any moment.

"I — I shot him," I reply through a thick layer of tears.

"You did, *malyshka*, and you got him. You did so well, and I am so proud of you."

"Is he — is he dead?"

"*Da*, angel. He's dead."

"And Sergei?"

"We will never see the likes of him again," Andrei assures me, his hand reaching down to rub my pregnant belly. "Our son will be born into a much safer world now."

"Oh, Andrei!" I gush, burying my face in his strong chest. He strokes the back of my head, gently weaving his fingers in and out of my blonde hair.

"I promise you things will be different now. We don't have to live in fear anymore. I'm going to protect us, and I'm never leaving you again."

We cling to each other this way for what feels like an eternity, simply soaking in each other's presence, breathing in a shared relief. I never want to let him go.

"*Ya tebya lyublyu*," I mumble into his shirt.

"I love you, too."

"Smile, Max!"

Andrei stands in front of us holding his iPhone, the camera flash lighting up and making the ten-month-old baby in my arms blink in confusion. I beam at the camera, tickling him to make him giggle. An infectious, delighted peal of laughter comes out of his little mouth, causing both Andrei and me to burst into laughter, too.

We're sitting on a woolly blanket in Central Park, the three of us bundled up in thick sweaters, mittens, and scarves. My little son's chubby, cherubic face is all rosy-cheeked from the brisk cold, so I reach into the diaper bag to retrieve his knit beanie with ear flaps. He hates the hat, I know, but the last thing we need is a sick baby on our hands. Especially since we are just about to leave on a trip tomorrow!

"Oh, that's a good one," Andrei says, grinning.

267

Sometimes it still catches me off-guard to see him looking this way — so happy and carefree. He used to smile only rarely, and when he did, it was a tentative, fleeting expression. Like he was afraid to be happy. But nowadays he's almost always smiling, laughing, making silly faces and sounds to entertain baby Maxim.

I didn't know it was possible to love anyone as much as I love my husband and son. And I never knew just how much happiness I could squish into my life.

"Was he looking at the camera this time?" I ask, coming around to lean on Andrei's shoulder and look at the iPhone screen.

"*Nyet*, looking at his mama, as usual." Andrei turns to kiss me on the cheek before doing the same to Max, who giggles again and reaches for his daddy's face.

"You wanna go to daddy?" I coo, hugging Max close.

"Da-da," he mumbles, his dark eyes crinkling up with delight at the mention of his father. The two of them are like two peas in a pod, totally fascinated by each other. Andrei takes Max from my arms and lifts him up, swinging him around in a circle while the baby laughs hysterically. My husband looks at Max with such tenderness and enchantment, like he's the most wonderful creature on the planet. And Max often stares wide-eyed at his daddy, scarcely blinking, totally entranced by his every move. I can already tell that Andrei is his hero.

But he loves me, too. I'm his comfort. I'm the one he wants when he cries, when he's hungry, when he's scared. Andrei is the fun one, and I'm the safety blanket. We suit our roles very well, I've discovered. When I first met Andrei, I never would have imagined this side of him: so gentle and sweet.

Sometimes I feel like my life is too good to be true. But it's totally real, and it's mine.

"So what time are we leaving in the morning?" I ask, leaning forward to take a strawberry out of the picnic basket and pop it into my mouth.

"I'm thinking around eight. So we have enough time to arrive in your hometown before Isaiah's piano lesson," Andrei replies, retrieving a strawberry and offering it to Max. The baby takes it excitedly and starts pulling the little green leaves off the top with inexplicable glee.

"I can't believe how fast he's growing up," I say, shaking my head. "Seems like just yesterday Isaiah was a baby, himself."

"And now he's an uncle," Andrei says, smiling.

I grin at the idea of my eight-year-old brother being an uncle. "Crazy."

After extensive research and intel, Andrei managed to track down my parents and Isaiah. They moved a county over from where I grew up, picking a new place to start over. Sure enough, Andrei found out through some particularly crafty sleuthing that my parents have been telling everyone that I moved to South America to be a missionary. They have no intentions of reaching out to me — I am essentially dead to them.

Honestly, even though it still hurts a little sometimes, I've gotten over that betrayal. My happiness with my current situation far outweighs my angst over what happened in the past. I no longer miss my mother and father. But I did miss my brother. Andrei couldn't stand to see me suffering, and he knew how badly I wanted Isaiah to meet his new nephew.

Last month was the first time I got to see my little brother since the day of our wedding. It took a lot of secretive planning, as well as a hefty pinch of kismet, to pull it off. It just so happens that my best friend and ballet instructor Sonya has a friend named Peter who teaches piano lessons in upstate New York. Since my old teacher retired years ago and my family was new to their area, I knew my parents would be on the hunt for a piano teacher for Isaiah.

So Andrei talked to Sonya who talked to Peter, who surreptitiously put himself forward as a private piano tutor, advertising himself as a man who specializes in hymns. It didn't take long for Jan and Arnold to sign up for Peter's services. And it wasn't long after that when Peter told Andrei he would be more than happy to facilitate a secret visit.

Overjoyed at the thought of being reunited, however temporarily, with Isaiah, I said yes and jumped at the opportunity. So last month we took a drive up north to see Isaiah during his piano lesson. I made him swear not to tell our parents, and he's old enough to know how serious the situation is, at least on some level. I think he understands that if he tells anyone about the meetings, our parents will only try that much harder to keep us apart.

Tomorrow, we are going back up there to visit him for a second time. And after that, we are catching a plane to Madrid! It will be my first time out of the country. Actually, it will be my first time ever even leaving the state of New York! We're going on a month-long tour of Europe, hitting Spain, France, Italy, and Switzerland before jetting up to Siberia for a short visit to Andrei's hometown of Yakutsk. It will be blisteringly cold there, of course, but he assures me that we will be perfectly fine. After all, there are lots and lots of people who live there year-round! I'm excited to see where my husband grew up. I know he will have to confront a lot of difficult memories, but with me beside him, I think it will be a cathartic experience.

Besides, Sonya will be meeting up with us there to see her mother for the first time in many, many years, and I cannot wait to see that reunion!

"Do you think we have enough winter clothes for Max?" I ask, biting my lip.

Andrei shrugs and lifts an eyebrow, a mischievous look crossing his face.

"We could always take him shopping in Europe."

I beam at him. "Europe," I breathe dreamily. "I never thought I would leave my hometown, much less travel the world!"

"And I never thought I would have a wife or a baby," Andrei says. "I never thought I could possibly have this kind of life."

"Then that makes two of us," I add, reaching over to take his hand.

He lifts my hand to his lips and kisses it, causing Max to make a delighted gurgling noise.

All three of us laugh, snuggled together under the sunny skies, a colorful life full of love and adventure ahead. I can't wait.

* * *

DON'T MISS out on the rest of the Hitman Series by Alexis Abbott! Now available on all ebook retailers.

*Owned by the Hitman*
*Ebook | Audiobook | Paperback*

*Sold to the Hitman*
*Ebook | Audiobook | Paperback*

*Saved by the Hitman*
*Ebook | Paperback*

*Captive of the Hitman*
*Ebook | Paperback*

*Stolen from the Hitman*
*Ebook | Paperback*

*Hostage of the Hitman*
*Ebook | Paperback*

*Taken by the Hitman*
*Ebook | Paperback*

ALSO BY ALEXIS ABBOTT

**Romantic Suspense:**

ALEXIS ABBOTT'S BOUND TO THE BAD BOY SERIES:

Book 1: Bound for Life

Book 2: Bound to the Mafia

Book 3: Bound in Love

ALEXIS ABBOTT'S HITMEN SERIES:

Owned by the Hitman

Sold to the Hitman

Saved by the Hitman

Captive of the Hitman

Stolen from the Hitman

Hostage of the Hitman

Taken by the Hitman

The Hitman's Masquerade (Short Story)

ROMANTIC SUSPENSE STANDALONES:

Criminal

Ruthless

Innocence For Sale: Jane

Reclaiming His Girls

Sights on the SEAL

Rock Hard Bodyguard

Abducted

Vegas Boss

I Hired A Hitman

Killing For Her

The Assassin's Heart

**Romance:**

Falling for her Boss (Novella)

Most Wanted: Lilly (Novella)

Bound as the World Burns (SFF)

**Erotic Thriller:**

THE DANGEROUS MEN SERIES:

The Narrow Path

Strayed from the Path

Path to Ruin

## ABOUT THE AUTHOR

Alexis Abbott is a Wall Street Journal & USA Today bestselling author who writes about bad boys protecting their girls! Pick up her books today if you can't resist a bad boy who is a good man, and find yourself transported with super steamy sex, gritty suspense, and lots of romance.

She lives in beautiful St. John's, NL, Canada with her amazing husband.

## CONNECT WITH ALEXIS

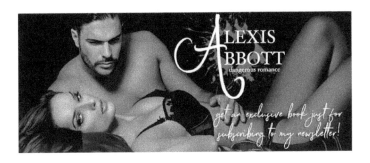

Get an EXCLUSIVE book, **FREE** just as a thank you for signing up for my newsletter! Plus you'll never miss a new release, cover reveal, or promotion!

http://alexisabbott.com/newsletter

facebook.com/abbottauthor

twitter.com/abbottauthor

instagram.com/alexisabbottauthor

bookbub.com/authors/alexis-abbott

pinterest.com/badboyromance

CPSIA information can be obtained
at www.ICGtesting.com
Printed in the USA
LVHW040823200723
752995LV00003B/40

CPSIA information can be obtained
at www.ICGtesting.com
Printed in the USA
BVHW030249190421
605284BV00015B/409